Meet me in Paris

Visit www.booksurge.com to order additional copies.

LuANN
MARSHALL

Meet me in Paris

2007

Meet me in Paris

This Book Is Dedicated To My Husband, Stephen. With You, I Traveled To Germany And France And Fell In Love With The People, History, And Culture Of These Countries. With Your Expertise In The Airline Industry, You Helped Me To Take The Reader Directly Into The Cockpit. Without Your Support And Belief In Me, This Book Would Still Be Wandering In My Mind And Not On The Written Page. I Thank You From The Bottom Of My Heart For All You Give To Me, And For That, I Honor You.

CHAPTER ONE

N adia Zeller looked up at the clock tower and realized she was late for the train. She was window-shopping after work and had lost track of the time. She raced into the doors of the main station. She had promised Mama she would be home for dinner tonight. Down the stairs she went, hoping she had not missed the Hanau-Steinheim 7:03 train departure. Just as she reached the platform, the train came to a stop at the station. She was relieved to have kept her promise.

She boarded the train car and settled into the seat her father had shown her to sit on during her practice trip into Frankfurt. She loved riding on the train, and when she became a teenager, Nadia begged her father to let her travel to Frankfurt for the day with her friends. But it wasn't until she turned fifteen that he felt she was old enough to travel alone without her family.

On her fifteenth birthday, she was thrilled when her father let her purchase her own ticket and board the train by herself. Actually, she wasn't alone on her first trip into the city because Papa traveled on the same train. He was there to see how she navigated her way home. Once he was satisfied that she could handle the train herself, the practice was over and she could travel alone. Papa would be proud that four years later she still selected her location wisely. "Find a seat, Nadia, where you can see the most people. It's very important," Papa insisted, "to be aware of your surroundings at all times."

The train moved quickly from the city lights into the darkness of the countryside. With each stop, the cars became less occupied. A young boy sitting across the aisle was sleeping with his head against the window. He was familiar to her. Every night he slept, but never failed to awaken just before his stop. Nadia had seen him board at the main station as she did each evening after work. His cloth jacket seemed more tattered than when she had first noticed him months before, but otherwise, he looked the same. He was predictable. Quiet. Sad, she thought. He carried a different fruit each day. Today he had an apple and a book. He only slept, never eating the fruit and never reading the book he held close to him. Mama said that everyone has a story, and Nadia wondered just what his story was.

Lights flashed quickly as the train moved in and out of each station. His stop was approaching, and she always worried that she must wake him. Soon he began to stir. He stretched his shoulders and made his way to the door. He dropped his glove and bent down to pick it up, and their eyes met. She smiled at him and caught a glimpse of his sad, brown eyes, but he looked away quickly as he stepped off the train. Again, he had awakened in time. It was a mystery to her that he never missed his stop.

Thirty minutes later, she walked from the train station back to her life, her family, and her home. She looked up and saw lace curtains in the second floor window. Directly below was the kitchen window, and through the glass she could see her mother, Isabella, busy preparing the evening meal. Before taking the job in Frankfurt, Nadia had helped her mother prepare the food. Now, she left early in the morning to catch the train and didn't return until the early evening.

Up the steps and into the door she went, hurrying back to the kitchen. She wrapped a clean apron around her small waist and kissed Mama hello. It was Nadia's favorite part of the day, where in the kitchen she would tell Mama all about her adventures in the city. Mama always had time for Nadia, but tonight there was little time for such things. Papa had called earlier to say that he was bringing guests for dinner, and Mama was preparing a special meal for the occasion.

"Nadia," said Mama, "help me to finish the table before Papa gets home. I have fresh flowers for the center." Mama enjoyed fine things, especially linens and flowers. Papa loved to bring floral bouquets home to Mama just to see the glow on her face. Mama always placed them on her dining table in her best crystal vase for all to enjoy. "You can serve goulash to a king, Nadia, if you place one beautiful rose on the table," Mama once told her.

Papa's boss was coming tonight, along with his wife, Hula. Nadia's father, George Zeller, had been working for Oskar Schiller as long as she could remember, and he had been very good to her father. Mr. Schiller was a kind man. He was tall, with white hair and a warm smile for everyone. He always wore fine business suits and carried a pipe, although he rarely lit it. She looked forward to seeing him, but she was not happy that his wife was joining him. Hula was a quiet, stern-looking woman who never smiled. In fact, she rarely spoke to anyone but Oskar, and with him it was with a sharp tongue. She made Nadia feel uncomfortable, but Mama explained that there were many different types of people in the world, and Nadia must accept everyone and not judge them. Still, Nadia didn't like the way Hula looked at her or her mama.

Hula was also tall, but very thin with sharp features. Her expression rarely changed from a disappointed frown, except when she looked at her son, Nicolas. *Nicolas! I wonder if he's coming?* Nadia felt giddy just thinking about him. She had had a crush on him ever since she was a little girl, and the feelings were much stronger now than ever.

Soon after Papa arrived, there came a knock on the door. "Come in. Come in, Mr. Schiller. So happy to have you in my home again."

Isabella came from the kitchen, drying her hands and removing her apron to receive their guests. "Welcome, Mr. Schiller. Are you alone? We were expecting Mrs. Schiller as well."

"Hula has been delayed, but she'll be joining us in a few minutes. Nicolas will be bringing her." Isabella took Mr. Schiller's hat and coat and hurried to place another seat at the table.

Nicolas was the Schillers' only son, and tall like his parents. He had dark hair like his mother and the kind, deep brown eyes of his father. When Isabella came back to the kitchen, she told Nadia that Nicolas was coming for dinner.

Nicolas. Just the sound of his name made Nadia's heart race. They had been out together several times since Nadia graduated from school, but she had never revealed to Mama just how interested she was in him. Only her two best friends, Anna Lese and Marcella, knew how she felt about him. She had confided in them about every conversation she had with Nicolas. She even told them about their first kiss and how he always brought her sweetheart roses when he took her out for the evening. They were her favorite flower, and she had saved every petal he gave to her. Silly, but she had a dream that one day they would be married and those petals would be strewn along the path she would take to walk toward her beloved Nicolas.

For a moment she was caught up in her daydream, then she glanced up from her work in the kitchen and noticed Mama looking over at her, smiling.

"I see your smile, Mama. You think I'm interested in Nicolas. He's too old for me, Mama, he's Alexander's friend. And besides," Nadia said playfully, "I found someone in the city that interests me."

Mama didn't think too kindly of that remark. "Who interests you, Nadia? I haven't seen or heard of him before now! Go wash up. You'll be joining us for dinner and you'll pay special attention to Nicolas. A girl couldn't do better than a kind young man like him."

Nadia took off her apron and went upstairs to her room. She was nineteen and Mama still spoke to her like she was a child. But she was too excited to be annoyed. *First news of Hula for dinner, and now Nicolas will be coming, too.* She looked at herself in the mirror. Her auburn hair had been pulled back for work today, but for dinner she decided to let it down. It fell past her shoulders in long, soft waves. *Nicolas once said he liked her hair down.*

Why did she have to make up a story about someone in the city? Mama would be full of questions after the guests left.

She opened her dresser drawer and looked at the picture taken last year at her graduation party. It had been a very special night. Nicolas paid a lot of attention to her, and he even had this picture taken of the two of them. Later that evening, he kissed her goodnight, handed her the photo, and said, "Keep this for our family album." Then he grinned and walked toward his car. *Family album! Was he joking, or could it be that he had the same feelings for her as she had for him?*

After taking one last look at herself in the hallway mirror, she took a deep breath before heading downstairs. *My heart is beating so fast! Why does Nicolas always affect me this way?*

CHAPTER TWO

Nadia came downstairs to find laughter coming from the front room. Nicolas and Hula had arrived and Mama was greeting them. Nadia had been working so much that she hadn't seen Nicolas for the past few weeks, and he had not lost his good looks. He winked at her, and she felt a stir inside. Nicolas always affected her that way. When he looked at her, she felt beautiful. Soon, that good feeling passed as Hula turned her attention to Nadia.

Hula was obviously disappointed to find Nadia at home. "Little Nadia," said Hula. "I didn't know you would be here. Your mother tells me that Madame Trist employs you. Doesn't she provide a room for you in Frankfurt?"

"Actually, Mrs. Schiller, Madame Trist employs me during the day to handle her affairs. The evenings and weekends are my own." Hula ignored Nadia's response as usual.

Everyone commented, except Hula, of course, that the house was filled with the aroma from Mama's good cooking. Dinner was ready and everyone was seated. Mama had prepared Mr. Schiller's favorite *sauerbraten* and *kartoffelklösse*. She had soaked the meat in brine overnight for the best flavor and took extra time making her delicious potato dumplings. She enjoyed pleasing her guests, and Mr. Schiller was thrilled to sit at her table.

"You spoil me, Isabella, with my favorite meal. Can I be so lucky that I smell apples baking?"

"Of course, Mr. Schiller, you'll have *apfel-küchen* for dessert."

George was proud of how Isabella's cooking made Mr. Schiller so happy. He had a good job at the bank working for him and wanted to continue as long as he could. A loose chain had injured his leg at the factory when Nadia was a little girl. George could no longer stand comfortably without a cane. When Mr. Schiller heard of his injury, he hired him to keep books at the bank, which allowed George to sit at a desk most of the day. Eventually, Mr. Schiller gave him more responsibility and, at times, left him in charge while he was away. He felt a great sense of gratitude toward Mr. Schiller and, although he was his boss, he had come to consider him a great friend.

Over the years, Mr. Schiller had grown fond of Isabella, her son Alexander, and little Nadia as though they were family, but Hula's jealousy of the beautiful Isabella and her lovely daughter had been the source of many arguments over the years. Isabella was a beautiful woman, with wavy auburn hair, which she kept up in a twist. She had pale, smooth skin and deep brown eyes, and her daughter looked just like her. She had a warm, kind spirit about her, and had made many friends throughout her fifty years in their small village.

Although Hula was cold toward Isabella and Nadia, Isabella was always gracious to both Hula and Oskar. Isabella was especially fond of Nicolas. She thought often about the young man. *How could sweet Nicolas come from such a bitter mother?*

Nadia ignored Mrs. Schiller's silence and followed her mother's lead to sit down at the table. Nicolas couldn't take his eyes off Nadia. She had become even more beautiful since he last saw her. She had a lovely softness to her face, like her mother, and the same warmth toward others.

"Nadia," Nicolas said, "tell me about Madame Trist. I know she was married to a famous artist named Christof Werner Trist. Is it true her husband died and left her a fortune? Father has been trying to get his hands on their money since they opened the gallery in Frankfurt."

"Nic! Watch what you say," said his father. "I only wish for her business to come through our bank."

"Don't worry, Father. I didn't mean it in a bad way. I just want to know more about Nadia's work."

Nadia smiled as she thought of her employer. "Yes, Madame Trist is a wealthy woman. But she's also kind and very fair. She's so beautiful, inside and out. And she's very smart about business. I enjoy working for her. She misses her husband tremendously, and does good things with her fortune. Just last week she made a large contribution to a children's ballet company in Frankfurt. She's a wonderful person, Nicolas. Sometimes I feel so sorry for her, though. You know, having lost the love of her life in such a tragic way."

Nicolas felt badly for the way he had talked about Madame Trist. Having been reminded of what had happened to her husband, he was eager to change the subject.

"So, what do you hear from Alex?"

Papa told him about his son's recent achievements at the private school in London, where he had been teaching for the past two years. Fortunately, his schedule allowed him to come home twice a year to see his family, and when he did come home, he and Nicolas spent time together.

While Papa was speaking to Nicolas, Mr. Schiller was filling his plate and covering his food with Mama's tangy gravy. George was proud to serve his boss such a fine meal. Hula barely touched her food, commenting that it was too rich and heavy to eat at this late hour.

Throughout dinner, Nadia and Nicolas talked about their work, their friends, and many other topics while Isabella and George listened. George looked over at his wife and winked, and she was a little bewildered by it. He seemed to know something she didn't know, but it wasn't the time or place to ask about it.

After dinner, Mr. Schiller asked George to come with him to the outside path so they could speak privately. Once they were alone, Mr. Schiller surprised him with his news.

"I'm going to train Nic to take my place at the bank. He'll be your boss soon." Mr. Schiller sighed, as though he was relieved to get this information out to George. "He'll need your help along the way."

"Of course, Mr. Schiller, I'll help him, but why are you leaving?"

"Retiring, George. I'm tired and weak. I need rest. I don't feel Nic can manage without you. He sometimes moves too quickly without thinking first. He needs to know he can come to you for help."

"Nicolas is a fine young man with a good education, Mr. Schiller. He will do well."

Oskar put his hand on George's arm. "Thank you, George, I knew I could count on you."

Hula had been speaking quietly with Nicolas in the front room while Isabella and Nadia finished the dishes. The men had returned from the path and were sitting on the steps outside the front door. Nadia took off her apron and joined Nicolas in the living room. She looked out the window and could tell something had happened. Papa was sitting quietly. Mr. Schiller held his pipe, but it wasn't lit. They both stared into the street.

Nicolas excused himself from his mother, thanked Mrs. Zeller for the fine meal, and asked Nadia to take a walk with him. Nadia looked at Mama, who nodded back with approval.

Nadia said she needed to go upstairs to get a sweater, but in fact, she needed time to catch her breath. Her heart was beating fast with excitement about being alone with Nicolas again. Even though she knew Mama suspected as much, Nadia had never revealed her true feelings to anyone. *Maybe tonight I'll tell Nicolas that I'm in love with him!*

She came downstairs and tried to act as though she wasn't jumping up and down inside to be alone with him again. They excused themselves and left through the kitchen door. Isabella found herself alone with Hula, but couldn't engage her in any conversation because the bitter woman was preoccupied trying to hear what the men were saying outside.

Nadia and Nicolas walked for some time before speaking, but they were holding hands before they even left her street.

"Nadia," said Nicolas, "my father is ill. He's retiring."

"Oh, Nicolas, I'm sorry he's sick."

"I'll be taking his place at the bank."

"How do you feel about this, Nicolas? You just graduated from the university last year. Are you prepared to take on such a large responsibility?"

"Of course I am. With your father's experience and my ideas, we should be fine. And my father will be there if I need to consult with him. Remember, I've worked at the bank ever since I was old enough to be put on the payroll."

Nadia thought of the years her father had worked at the bank and wondered how he would feel about working for such a young man.

"You can help me too, Nadia."

"Of course I would help if I could, but I already have a job that I love. Working for Madame Trist is so exciting. Crazy, mad exciting! I can't wait to see what each day brings. Banking would be so boring to me."

Nicolas's heart was beating out of his chest and he couldn't wait any longer to speak these words. "Nadia, will you marry me?"

Nadia stopped walking and turned to look into his eyes. She could see on his face he was serious. "Oh, Nicolas, I'm honored, but we don't know each other well enough to marry."

His face dropped with disappointment. "We've known each other since childhood."

"I...I can't be married. I want to go to college, and my job with Madame Trist is very important to me. Besides, your mother stares at me with disgust. She would never accept anyone as your wife, especially me."

"I don't live for my mother, Nadia. I want to live for us and our future."

"But Nicolas, you don't know me."

"I've known you since we were children and watched you grow to become a beautiful and caring young woman. I've been patient until the time was right to tell you that I'm in love with you."

Nadia's eyes welled with tears. *She couldn't believe he loved her, too.*

"Remember when I asked you to marry me in the park? I'm that same boy who loved you back then."

"We were kids playing house. What you're asking me now is real."

"Look into my eyes, Nadia. I've dreamed of the day we could be together. We can have a good life, baby, I promise."

Nadia didn't know what to say. *It was one thing to fall in love with him, but he's proposing marriage! Was she ready for marriage?* She was six years younger than Nicolas. Her mind flashed with faces of her family. *Mama, Papa, Alex, they would be so happy. But would she be happy with Nicolas?*

He pulled her close and whispered in her ear. "This is my dream, Nadia. In time, you will come to love me as much as I do you. I promise to make you happy."

Tears streamed down Nadia's face. Just moments ago, Nadia knew who she was, and it was not Mrs. Nicolas Schiller. Nadia pulled away from him. "Nicolas, I'm not in love with you. We're friends. My father works for your father."

"That's not true, Nadia. You do have feelings for me. You love me. I see it in your eyes when we're together. C'mon, give us a chance, my love," he pleaded.

Nadia had turned her back to him. *Why did I say I didn't love him?*

Nicolas thought for a moment before he spoke again. "If you marry me, your father will have job security, Nadia. As long as he has his health, I promise he will work."

Nadia knew her father worried about providing for his family since his accident. She could relieve his worry by saying yes to Nicolas's offer. She knew he would make a good life for her, and her parents would have a secure future.

Besides, she was madly in love with him, and it was getting harder to resist her feelings.

She turned back to face him. "Even if I agreed to marry you, Hula would be a problem. Your mother hates me, Nicolas. She hates my mother, too."

"My mother is very difficult to understand, but I can handle her. She wants only the best for me, and that's you. I'll give her an ultimatum. She'll accept our love or we'll not be in her life."

Nadia continued to deny her feelings. "Our love? There is no such thing as our love, Nicolas! I can't be in love with you or anyone else. I plan to attend the university. Papa worked hard to provide this opportunity for me to have an education. It's my parent's dream for me to attend school in Frankfurt. With what they've saved, and the money I'm earning, I should be able to start classes next year."

"Nadia, are you listening to me? Forget about everyone else's dreams and let's make our own life together. I'll provide for us. You can go to school now. I'll guarantee a job for your father." He cupped her beautiful face in his gentle hands and looked deeply into her brown eyes. "Nadia. Listen to me. It's time. I'm here for you now. I can make all of this happen."

She could feel his love and passion for her. Her dreams of a life with Nicolas had come true. Secretly, Nadia had always known she would have a wonderful life if she married him.

"Once again, I'm asking you to be my wife."

Nicolas took Nadia's right hand and placed a ring on her finger. She had never seen such a beautiful diamond ring! Mama wore a thin silver band that Papa had given to her on her sixteenth birthday when he proposed marriage to the young Isabella. This ring had round pavé and bezel-set diamonds that glittered in delicate swirls of gold.

Tears fell from her eyes as he kissed the ring on her finger. "My grandmother gave this ring to me before she died, Nadia. She asked me to place it on the finger of my true love. Even then, I told her it would be you. You remember her, don't you?"

"I remember her. She was lovely."

"She was very fond of you."

Nadia couldn't believe she was wearing such a beautiful heirloom ring. She thought about his grandmother, and how much she had loved her only grandson.

"Nadia, your mama will be happy, too. I will be a dutiful son to Isabella and George."

He pulled her close to his chest with his arms tight around her. Nadia stayed quiet for some time.

He is right, she thought. *Mama has always been fond of Nicolas and will be proud to have him as a son in the family. He's a good man. Papa can live his years without worry. Nicolas and Alex have been best friends since childhood.* Although she refused to admit it to him, she had loved him since she was a young girl, running alongside of him and her brother in the playground.

He held her close and waited for what seemed to be an eternity.

Suddenly, Nadia began to smile through her tears.

"Does this mean your answer is yes?"

"My answer is...yes!"

Nicolas lifted Nadia and twirled her around in his arms. They both laughed as they nearly tumbled before coming to a stop. "You won't regret this, Nadia. We'll be happy. We'll buy our dream house, give our parents lots of grandchildren, and grow old together."

"Here, Nicolas? Where I can stay close to my family?"

"Of course, here. I love our parents and my work is here."

Calm came over Nadia when she thought of having a family of her own and living close to Mama and Papa. *Nicolas would be a wonderful father. Maybe this was to be her life after all. Mrs. Nicolas Schiller. Nadia Schiller.*

"Come on, Nadia. Let's go and tell our parents."

On the walk home, they talked and laughed with excitement. They passed by the playground where they used to meet together when they were younger and dreamed of their own children playing there one day.

As they neared her home, she thought of what her parents would say. They would be thrilled with the news. She didn't even care about the way Hula would glare at her when Nicolas announced the engagement.

But what will Madame Trist say when I tell her I'm getting married?

They finally reached the house and slipped back in through the kitchen door. Their parents were in the living room enjoying coffee and Mama's delicious apple cake. Nicolas kissed Nadia and then asked if she was ready. She nodded, and they joined their parents in the living room.

"Family, we have news!"

Their parents looked up from their conversation, waiting to hear what Nicolas had to say.

"Nadia and I are getting married!"

Nadia looked at her parents. Mama started to cry, and Papa beamed with pride.

"Mama, Papa, I believe Nicolas and I can make a good life together. Please give us your blessing to marry."

An uncomfortable quiet fell over the room for just a brief moment, then laughter and hugs and tears flowed in celebration of their engagement. "My baby," said Mama, "I only wish you happiness. You surprised me with this announcement, but I've always known that Nicolas was in love with you. Perhaps before you even knew it yourself."

Papa shook Nicolas's hand, which then led to a hug. Papa looked at Nadia and put his hand over his heart. "Nicolas came to me yesterday and asked for my permission to marry you. I didn't know at the time that he would be able to provide for you, but I knew he was true in his feelings. Just like I was when I asked for your mother's hand in marriage. For that reason, I gave him my blessing."

"George! You didn't tell me of this proposal."

"Some things are best left unsaid, Mama. We can't stand in the way of love." Mama hugged Papa and then Nadia, and before long Nicolas came into the embrace. Her parents admired the beautiful ring their daughter was wearing, and listened as Nicolas told them of his grandmother's wish. It was such an incredible moment that Nadia almost forgot that the Schillers were standing quietly together. Nadia pulled away from her parents, and Nicolas took her hand and they walked together toward Oskar and Hula.

"Mother, I already told Father of my plans to marry Nadia. I'm asking for your blessing. Please understand that whatever you say, it will not change my plans. I love her, Mother."

Hula's expression softened as Nicolas spoke to her. She knew that to keep her son she must accept his decision. Hula opened her arms and held her son close and whispered to him that he had her blessing.

She felt like choking on her words, but it just simply wasn't the right time to take action to prevent this ridiculous union. Hula hugged Nadia, and as they embraced, she thought of her strategy to stop this wedding from taking place and getting that ring back where it belonged. *Why didn't she know that Oskar's mother had given such a valuable ring to Nicolas?*

Oskar, surprised at his wife's reaction, knew better. *Tomorrow, Hula will bring trouble to the couple and to me for not telling her of my talk with Nicolas.* Oskar dreaded going home with Hula tonight. But for his son, at this moment, he would forget his troubles and drink in celebration of Nadia and Nicolas's engagement and of moving one day closer to his retirement.

CHAPTER THREE

Hula was unusually quiet on the ride home. Oskar was relieved, but he knew it was only time until she blew up, and somehow he would be blamed for the marriage. She found a way to make him feel guilty over just about anything that happened in their lives. Oskar stared at the road ahead and thought about his life with Hula. Lines on his face from worry and stress made him look older than his seventy years. He had loved her once, but his domineering wife was never happy or satisfied with him.

He had waited many years to become a father. "Never a good time, Oskar," Hula would say. She was twelve years younger than her husband and waited until after they were married to tell him that she didn't want any children. She finally gave birth to a son years later for fear that she would lose Oskar with her constant nagging.

She devoted her life to Nicolas. He was home-schooled initially, and then attended a private academy for those who were fortunate enough to afford it. Throughout childhood, his best friend was Alexander Zeller, Nadia's older brother. Alexander attended public school, as did Nadia. His father had introduced Nicolas to the Zeller children one summer; from that point on, Nicolas couldn't wait until he could meet his friend Alexander at the park to play. His little sister, Nadia, was always with Alexander, and Nicolas enjoyed her company as well. Nicolas longed to be happy like Alexander and Nadia. Life for them seemed so fun and carefree. Mrs. Zeller watched her children play and enjoyed visiting with the other mothers. Nicolas's mother always sat away from everyone, reading her book and looking over her glasses at her son. Sometimes, Nicolas secretly wished he lived with their family instead of his own.

As they pulled into the driveway of their house, Hula finally spoke. "What makes you think that our son would marry such a twit? He hardly knows her, and her family is poor. For God's sake, what are you going to do about this, Oskar?"

He thought carefully and decided the best thing to do was to stay silent as long as he could. Fortunately for him, she continued to speak.

"It's your fault he's with that girl. You allowed him to be friendly with that family. I told you it would be a problem one day. I told you so."

Once inside the house, Oskar went into his study and pulled out a bottle from his desk. As he poured a much-needed drink, he leaned back in his chair, closed his eyes, and wondered how he could protect his son from what his wife was about to do.

CHAPTER FOUR

Nadia had a hard time falling asleep that night after Nicolas left, so she stayed on the phone with Anna Lese and Marcella until she felt tired. They were thrilled with her news, and couldn't wait to help her start making plans for the wedding. When she finally decided to lie down, she stared at the ring on her finger, thinking about how life would be with Nicolas.

When Papa locked up and went upstairs for bed, he noticed the light coming from Nadia's room. He opened the door and found her fast asleep. He watched her sleep for a moment, and thought about how quickly the days were passing by. Alexander was grown and had moved to London to teach, and now his little girl was getting married. He covered her with Mama's handmade quilt and kissed her goodnight on the forehead, just as he had done since she was a little girl. When he turned around, Isabella was standing in the doorway, smiling.

Even with tonight's events, Nadia still left her light on for her father to come by and turn off. When she and Alexander were growing up, Papa worked late at the factory. They always knew he was home if they awoke and found that their lights had been turned off.

In the morning, Nadia came downstairs and paused to watch Mama in the kitchen, cooking breakfast. She wondered how it would be for her mother once she married. Mama's arthritis had settled in her hands and hips, and getting around for her was becoming more difficult. Nadia had always helped Mama with the household chores. She wanted to live close by so she could keep an eye on both of her parents.

"Nadia, come in the kitchen and have breakfast with me."

"Good morning, Mama!" Nadia kissed Mama on the forehead. "I don't have much time. I'm taking the early train so I can speak with Madame Trist before she gets involved in her morning phone calls. I want to tell her that I'm engaged."

Nadia thought to herself for a moment. "I'm a little nervous, but I'm sure she'll be happy for me. I really like her, Mama. I like working for her, too. I want to reassure her that I plan to continue working for her until she closes the Frankfurt gallery."

"Madame Trist must be a wonderful person, Nadia."

"Oh, Mama, she's amazing. I've never met anyone like her. She's strong and beautiful. And she has a sharp business sense. I'm learning so much from her."

Nadia poured them both a cup of coffee and encouraged Mama to sit down with her. They both sat quietly for a few moments. "Mama, what are you thinking? You look so serious."

"I'm wondering about Hula this morning."

"What about her?"

"Did you see the look on her face last night when they left? She wasn't happy."

"Mama, she's *never* happy. Don't worry about her. She'll just have to adjust to our marriage. Besides, Nicolas has promised me that she won't be a problem. Look at the time!" Nadia kissed Mama and rushed upstairs to finish getting ready for work. Soon, she was out the door to meet the morning train.

Isabella could see her from the kitchen window. She watched until Nadia turned the corner and she lost sight of her girl. She couldn't help but be worried. If Hula had her way, the marriage might never happen.

Earlier that morning in Frankfurt, the doorman had waited anxiously for Madame Trist to leave for her morning walk. Every day, he enjoyed her smile as he opened the glass door for her. She had never disappointed him, always looking at him directly with a warm smile and the words *bonjour* and *merci*. He imagined Madame Trist at her Paris apartment. *Did she smile at the doorman there and treat him as kindly?* Since the death of Monsieur Trist, he was told that she would be leaving their apartment in Frankfurt once his gallery was closed. She was there to settle her late husband's affairs.

He watched as she crossed the busy street, wondering where her walk took her each day. She turned the corner, and he lost sight of her.

A few minutes later, Nadia arrived at the apartment building. She was to meet Madame Trist there that morning. The doorman recognized Nadia and told her that Madame Trist had not yet returned from her walk. That pleased Nadia because it gave her a chance to settle in before her boss returned.

Nadia was given a key to Madame Trist's apartment because there were many days that she worked from home instead of the gallery. She let herself in and reviewed the notes Madame Trist had left for her. She returned the calls on the list and wondered where Madame Trist could be, and then she remembered that it was she that had come in early that morning.

Gisela Trist finally arrived, and Nadia helped her with her coat. She wore beautiful clothes, and Nadia loved the feel of that particular ivory swing coat made of buttery leather.

Madame Trist could tell that Nadia was excited about something and she sat down with her assistant for a few minutes to chat.

"You're in early today, Nadia."

"Yes, yes, I am. I have something important to tell you before we get started."

"What is it?"

"I'm getting married! Nicolas asked me to marry him…and I said yes!"

Gisela was taken by surprise. It wasn't at all what she expected to hear. "I didn't even know you were dating, Nadia."

"Well, I know it sounds crazy, but please be happy for me. He's just wonderful and he'll make the best husband ever."

Gisela thought about that old saying, "What a difference a day makes." It certainly was true.

She smiled at Nadia. "Then, tell me about this wonderful man."

As Nadia spoke of her fiancé, Gisela poured them both a cup of tea. "I can't help but notice that lovely ring. It's an antique, isn't it?"

"Yes, it is. It belonged to his grandmother."

"Well, she had excellent taste. Now, how does this affect your future plans with work and college?"

"Of course, I'll continue working for you, Madame Trist, until you close the gallery. That's what we had planned anyway, that I would work for you until the project was finished. I still plan to attend the university next year, and, well, I just want you to know that nothing has changed between us. I love working for you."

Gisela couldn't help but smile at her enthusiasm. "What about our trip to New York, Nadia?"

Nadia almost forgot. "No problem. Nicolas is very supportive of my work." She made a note to herself on the pad in front of her. *I need to tell Nicolas about this.*

When she finished, Madame Trist stood up and reached for Nadia's hand. Nadia stood up with her. "Nadia, you look radiantly happy. If this is what you want, I'm happy for you." She hugged her for the first time, and Nadia was relieved. As she held the young girl, Gisela realized just how fond she had become of her assistant.

"Well, now, let's get busy, shall we?"

Nadia told her of the early morning messages and Madame Trist sat down at her desk to return her calls. Nadia was relieved to have Madame Trist's support, and she almost felt guilty feeling so happy when Madame Trist was still grieving for her beloved husband. She could see the sadness in her eyes whenever another painting was sold and shipped to a buyer.

At first, Gisela Trist had intended to sell the Frankfurt gallery, contents and all. But she found it more comforting to try and sell the paintings on their own, placing her late husband's work in the hands of buyers who enjoyed his talent. She had trained Nadia to sell the paintings in her absence, as she frequently traveled back home to oversee her affairs in Paris. Her schedule seemed overwhelming to Nadia, but Gisela found it less stressful to stay busy.

Nadia spent most of her days answering the phones and arranging shipping schedules. With the publicity of Madame Trist's arrival in Frankfurt, the paintings had begun to sell quickly and the details of each transaction kept Nadia busy. Thousands of dollars were paid for Christof's original oils. This fascinated Nadia, as she often ended up handling more money than she ever thought she would see at once.

Madame Trist finished her calls and they both walked down the street and around the corner to continue their workday at the gallery. Gisela watched as Nadia guided potential buyers through the artwork. When she had applied for the job, Gisela was concerned about Nadia's ability to associate with high-end clients. Besides, she had little experience, other than work at the church office during the summers and after school caring for several young children in her community. But she saw a hunger in young Nadia that she had once had inside of herself. Nadia wanted to learn and experience new things, and she had convinced Gisela to give her a chance. Since that time, she had done a wonderful job for her.

The phone rang, and before Nadia could excuse herself from the client, Madame Trist nodded that she would take the call. It was Hula Schiller.

"Yes, Mrs. Schiller. I simply won't be able to meet with you. Sorry, I'm traveling for the next few weeks. Perhaps my assistant can help you next week. After that, she'll be traveling, too."

Hula was annoyed with the delay. "Well, I would like to meet directly with you, Madame Trist."

"I'm flattered, Mrs. Schiller, but my assistant Nadia is more than qualified to show the paintings. I really must encourage you to meet with her, because waiting until we return from our trip may cause you to miss the opportunity to see many of my husband's works. They're going very quickly. In fact, I may be closing the Frankfurt gallery much sooner than I expected."

"How about this evening, Madame Trist? Would you be able to meet with me tonight, say, about seven o'clock?"

Gisela was becoming very annoyed with this woman, but since she was so persistent and seemed to know so much about her husband's paintings, she agreed to meet her at the gallery that night.

In the meantime, Nadia closed the sale of a painting so dear to Gisela's heart. It was of a young boy she and her husband had encountered on one of their weekend getaways. She still remembered his haunting, big brown eyes, and how Christof captured his stillness in the painting.

After the paperwork was completed, Nadia looked at Madame Trist for approval. She knew it was a favorite of hers, and, although she had already selected her personal choices for shipment to Paris, Nadia felt uncomfortable selling the piece. Gisela smiled and winked at her. All was well and the client was pleased with her choice.

"Nadia, I'm going to leave for a while. I'm meeting a client this evening, so I'll be back later. Just lock up if you have to leave before I return, but keep the spotlights on. I'll close up later this evening."

Before she left, Gisela opened her gold cosmetic case and used a lip brush to touch up her lips with a beautiful shade of red. The color matched her nail polish perfectly. Nadia watched as she walked out the door. Everything about Madame Trist fascinated her. She felt so fortunate to have met such an interesting woman.

The rest of the afternoon was busy between appointments and phone calls, but Nadia managed to leave the gallery in time to catch the train. The young boy on the train was getting more relaxed with Nadia. Today, he even smiled back at her when he exited at his stop.

As the train pulled into the Hanau-Steinheim station, Nadia gathered her briefcase and jacket. She was tired tonight. The afternoon had been hectic and Madame Trist had left her alone for hours. She wondered where she went, and with whom she was meeting tonight at the gallery.

Nadia settled in and went into the kitchen. Mama was busy preparing dinner. "Hello, Mama."

"Hello! Oh dear, you look exhausted. Come and sit for a minute. Dinner will be ready when Papa gets home."

"I must admit I am tired tonight. I was so busy today. The paintings are selling quickly, Mama. I heard her tell someone she might close the gallery sooner than she expected. It's crazy, the way they're selling. People from all over Europe are calling for prices. Some pieces are under bid. It's a lot to keep up with. Today, Madame Trist left me alone all afternoon. She has to work tonight."

"Tonight? I thought the gallery was closed in the evenings."

"It is, but someone called and made an appointment. Someone pushy, I understand, from the way Madame Trist was talking on the phone."

Nadia reached for a clean apron, but Mama stopped her. "No, not tonight. I can finish dinner myself, Nadia. Go wash up. Papa should be here any minute."

The aroma of sauerkraut and knockwurst met Papa at the door. "Mama, I'm home." Papa took off his hat and coat and rested his cane against the hall door.

"Go wash up," she answered. "Dinner is almost ready."

They all sat quietly and enjoyed Mama's cooking. After Mama and Nadia finished putting up the last dish, Nadia joined Papa on the sofa. She sat down next to him and leaned her head on his shoulder.

"What's wrong, little girl?"

"Nothing, Papa. I came to ask *you* that question."

"I'm old and tired. Now what's your excuse for such a sad expression at dinner?"

"Oh, Papa! I'm not sad…just thinking."

"About what?"

"So many things. Like going to America with Madame Trist. It's kind of overwhelming!"

By this time, Mama had removed her apron and settled in her chair to do some sewing. "Oh, America! You're still planning to go on this trip? What about your engagement to Nicolas? It seems to me that a wedding takes time and planning..."

"Oh, Mama, so that's what's on your mind. You hardly said anything at dinner."

"And just when is this wedding taking place?"

"I don't know. Nicolas and I will decide that. I think maybe a year from now, maybe a little longer than that. It depends on whether I have enough money saved to start school at the first of the year."

"Why is going to school so important to you? What about your husband, Nadia? A family?"

"Oh, Mama! I love you, but you are so old-fashioned. These days a girl needs an education whether or not she marries."

Papa looked up over his paper. "She's right, Mama."

"All I know is that a wonderful boy asked you to marry him, and you plan to put him on hold. He might not want you to spend years in school when you could be taking care of him instead."

Nadia tried to be patient with her parents, but she was getting upset at Mama's persistence. "Please, Mama. It's my life. Nicolas wants me to get an education. We've discussed it. It's settled." Nadia headed upstairs to call her fiancé.

Isabella looked up at her husband from her sewing and shook her head. "It's not right, George."

He knew when to stay out of it. He sighed and continued to read his paper.

CHAPTER FIVE

Hula made an excuse to be gone when Oskar came home. He was always relieved to find an evening when the house would be quiet, so he went straight home from the bank and took a nap.

Hula drove into Frankfurt and made sure to arrive right on time. She knocked on the window of the gallery and Madame Trist unlocked the door. "Mrs. Schiller?"

"Yes, Madame Trist. I'm pleased to meet you." Hula watched as Madame Trist relocked the doors. *Gisela Trist was even more beautiful in person.*

"Now, Mrs. Schiller, what is it that you would like to see?"

"Oh. Yes, well…something in a watercolor."

Gisela could see that this appointment was not going to go quickly. "I see. Let's take a walk over this way." Gisela began to show her husband's works from their island travels, taking a few moments to explain each piece to Mrs. Schiller.

After some time, Hula decided to make her move.

"Madame Trist, we know someone in common. Nadia Zeller. Nadia is a friend of my son, Nicolas Schiller. He works with my husband at the bank our family owns."

"Why, yes. I'm quite fond of Nadia."

"You said she's planning to travel to New York with you. Just how long will she be gone?"

"Mrs. Schiller, I'm sure that Nadia has discussed her plans with her family. Now about this painting, do you think it has the right dimensions for your husband's office?"

Hula was annoyed that Madame Trist did not answer her question. "No, in fact, it's too small. Much too small."

"Well then. What about *Sea Diamonds?* It's much larger and the pastel shades are so soothing to the eye."

"Actually, nothing seems to be what I need. I appreciate your time, but I must be on my way."

"Of course, Mrs. Schiller."

Hula put on her gloves and black leather coat.

"Oh, by the way, Mrs. Schiller, I'm sure whatever Nadia decides about her travel will be appropriate for both her and her fiancé. Your son is her fiancé, isn't he?"

Hula stopped at the door and looked back at Madame Trist. *How dare Nadia discuss her son with that woman!* "Goodnight, Madame Trist."

Gisela was happy to see her leave. She turned off the lights and locked up again. As she walked back to her apartment, she thought of Christof. *He would not have been so kind to the bitter woman.*

CHAPTER SIX

Christof Werner Trist had fallen madly in love with Gisela and their life together had been amazing. She had met Christof six years ago at the opening of his new art gallery in New York.

Gisela had flown to New York from Paris to visit with her parents, Bernhard and Katharina Sommer. Katharina was a great fan of Christof's work, and encouraged Gisela to join her at a party she was hosting in his honor Monday evening. Gisela usually spent her time in the theatre district, enjoying the shows and backstage gatherings, but since the theatres were dark that night, she agreed to join her parents and meet her mother's latest new artist at the gallery.

All eyes were on Gisela as she entered the rounded doorways. Her hair fell long against a cream silk suit by L'san. She was a favorite client of this French designer. Rarely did one see a woman at her young age of twenty-six in such feminine attire, with a matching silk hat, gloves, shoes, and handbag. Just like her mother, Gisela was a classic beauty with striking features. She had sky blue eyes and her pale blonde hair shimmered like diamonds. L'san loved to dress her and she wore his designs almost exclusively.

"Gisela, darling, I'm so glad you decided to join us." Katharina kissed her on both cheeks, took her daughter's hand, and led her to the guest of honor.

"Christof, dear, I would like you to meet Gisela." She looked at him and was immediately captivated by his presence. He was tall, and his skin was a golden tan as if he had spent weeks relaxing on the beach. His black hair, deep, penetrating eyes, and angular jaw line with just a touch of black beard growth almost took her breath away. *He was so unlike the other artists she had met before.*

"Mrs. Sommer, it is *my* pleasure. Gisela, I've heard so much about you." She smiled, now aware of the reason her parents had wanted her to join them this evening.

"I must say, Mr. Trist, I've admired the paintings my parents have purchased from you."

Christof tried to remain calm, but the sight of her made him shiver with excitement. "Shall we take a look at some of my new work?"

The rest of the evening they enjoyed each other's company, talking and laughing playfully. Bernhard and Katharina glanced at each other approvingly. Katharina had thought Christof would be a perfect match for her daughter, and from the looks of things tonight, she knew she was right.

From that night on, Christof and Gisela became inseparable. They were photographed everywhere they went. Gisela rarely came to the States, but when she did, society welcomed her with lavish parties and attention. Christof was less of a socialite, but knew the importance of these relationships when it came to his art. Away from the social scene, they spent their time at his loft, his favorite galleries, and walking in Central Park. Gisela loved to take long morning walks. They relaxed her and she used the time to prepare and think through her day's events. But these walks with Christof were much different. Hand in hand, they strolled through the paths laughing, talking, and becoming closer every day they spent together.

Once Gisela returned to Paris, Christof longed for her and begged her to move to New York, but Gisela loved Parisian life, and her boutique was enjoying a third successful year. So, to entice him to move to Paris, she found a beautiful, brightly lit second floor apartment overlooking the Seine, just perfect for showing Christof's paintings.

The following month, when he came to visit her in Paris, he saw the apartment she rented. Light came through the window, streaming across the room, and he knew this was where he was meant to be. At that moment, his future became clear to him. He would open another gallery in Paris and ask this beautiful woman to be his bride.

On a cool Paris evening, standing on a footbridge overlooking the River Seine, Christof held Gisela close to keep her warm, and they soon began to sway slowly, back and forth, in a rhythmic dance. She melted into his arms, hearing only him breathing softly into her ear. No music, no outside world, only the sound of his breathing and the beating of his heart against hers. Gisela never felt so safe. After what seemed to be a beautiful, private eternity, he spoke, ending their silence.

"I can't live another day without you by my side."

Gisela looked up into his eyes and spoke softly, as her own tears began to fall. "Christof, I feel the same as you...I can't bear for you to leave for New York tomorrow."

His life felt complete. "Marry me, Gisela."

Marriage? Christof had never spoken of marriage, but she was thrilled.

"Yes, yes, yes! I will marry you!"

They embraced, and then, suddenly, she thought of leaving the city she loved. "But your life is in New York, Christof. I can't possibly leave Paris. My business is here."

"I'll move to Paris. I'll open a gallery here and travel to New York when it's necessary."

"Are you sure, Christof? For me, you would do this for me?"

"For us." Gisela leaped into his arms and they kissed as he spun her around. When they stopped, Christof made the announcement to the inquisitive crowd that had gathered.

"This woman is my love, my life!" In typical Parisian style, the crowd applauded the young lovers.

By this time, the sun had set and the reflection of the city lights was breathtaking.

"Come, let's seal this with a kiss on top of the Eiffel Tower." Without warning, Christof began to run across the bridge and onto the avenue with Gisela in tow. As they came closer to the illuminated tower, they stopped running to take a breath. Soon, they gathered their senses and laughed at their childlike behavior. They walked hand in hand toward Rue de Rapp. They turned the corner and found a large crowd waiting in line to take the tour.

Gisela took Christof over to see the statue of Gustave Eiffel. She told him that Eiffel, an expert in metal construction, had also worked on the structural framework of the Statue of Liberty. Christof tried to contain his laughter as he saluted the bust of the mighty metal architect. "Monsieur Eiffel, I would like to introduce you to my bride to be, Gisela. I am Christof, a humble artist, and I have often painted your Lady Liberty. Now that I'll be living with my beloved in Paris, I must ask your permission to paint your towering treasure."

Gisela loved his playful side, and she laughed as he bowed at the golden face of Gustave Eiffel. Suddenly, a street vendor appeared with a variety of souvenirs. Gisela chose a miniature Eiffel Tower, gray metal with red shimmering stones. As Christof paid the young man, several older boys on bicycles raced through the crowd, alerting these illegal vendors that the police were on the way. As the boys scattered with the others to hide, he turned back to them and shouted, "Merci!"

Soon, the police walked through the crowd. Once the men in uniform passed through the tower area and exited toward the street, a mass of young boys appeared once again to go about their business of selling to the eager tourists. "This ballet, of sorts, continues around the clock between the young boys and the police," Gisela explained as she pointed out their favorite hiding places. "They sell these souvenirs at a better price than the gift shops do here."

The lines grew shorter and the couple decided to join the others and wait their turn to ride up into the tower. As promised, he held her close as they kissed and sealed their new covenant.

Christof was fascinated by the beauty and history of Paris, but as he looked at his love that evening, the sight of Gisela with the wind in her hair, struggling to keep her silk scarf in place, by far outshone all of the beauty beneath them.

CHAPTER SEVEN

Bernhard and Katharina were thrilled when Gisela told them
of her engagement to Christof. They were quietly hoping that
Gisela would move to New York, but they understood why she
and Christof would make their home in Paris. She loved the city, and it
provided a perfect background for Christof's artistic talent.

Gisela agreed to her parents' wish for an elaborate engagement
party, but she insisted that their wedding reflected the couple's love for
each other: quiet, powerful, and intimate. With the whirlwind of parties,
dinners, and family and friends' best wishes behind them, Gisela and
Christof kissed their families goodbye and boarded a flight to Athens.
There, they sailed off the coast of Mykonos one beautiful June morning
and vowed to love each other eternally.

They were one, basking in the sun by day and dancing barefoot in
the sand by night. Christof sketched his beautiful bride whenever he
had a chance, with the Aegean Sea in the background. He loved the
wonderful Mediterranean light. But his favorite sketch was of Gisela,
sitting on the terrace one evening looking up at the stars. He had worked
diligently to capture the moonlight's reflection on her hair and face.

They made love, laughed, and dreamed of their new life together as
husband and wife.

Gisela was the happiest she had ever been. When the honeymoon
was over, the couple focused on opening a Paris gallery.

Christof showered his wife with gifts, and she loved the little
packages he brought home to her, but the most treasured gift of all was
a portrait of his bride he secretly painted from the sketches he made
on their honeymoon. He christened it *Moonlight*, and presented it to his
beloved on their first anniversary.

Life for the Trist's was filled with love and laughter. Christof hired
a trusted friend to manage his New York commitments and eventually
found a curator for the Paris gallery. The two locations performed so
well that he decided to open a gallery in Frankfurt. This location was

immediately successful and he found a wonderful gentleman to manage the daily affairs. This enabled him to work out of their Paris home, just as they had planned. Between the two of them, they owned the three galleries and her shop, La Boutique de Gisela.

Their first years together were seamless. They traveled to events and buying trips as a couple and were rarely seen apart. They were a stunning pair and attracted many admirers. Christof stood tall, with his dark hair and European attire, and Gisela, a classic beauty, with long shimmering blonde hair and light blue eyes. Her clothing was exquisite, and her accessories were always on the cutting edge of fashion. She had an eye for design, and her clothing style reflected her taste in haute couture.

However, the time came when Christof found himself needing to be in New York on a date that conflicted with their Paris gallery schedule. They decided that he would go ahead to New York and she would stay and oversee the gallery event, then join him the following week. Her parents were thrilled to have their daughter home for a visit. They hadn't seen her since they vacationed in Paris the previous year. They also adored Christof, and welcomed the opportunity to spend some time alone with their son-in-law before Gisela arrived in New York.

When the day came to travel to New York, Christof reluctantly boarded the flight without her. He waited to leave home until the last possible moment to catch his flight and still felt rushed. He made one last call to Gisela before they took off. "Baby, I miss you already," he said.

"I miss you, too. Love you, want you, need you."

Christof settled in his first class seat and looked out the window as the plane taxied to the runway. Once airborne, he worked to finalize the proposal that he would present to potential investors and forwarded a copy to Gisela. After the evening meal service, he leaned his seat back and slept for the remainder of the flight. He arrived at JFK just in time to shower and change at the loft before his 8:30 breakfast meeting with his accountant at the offices of Steinbach, Keller and Mahr.

It was a glorious morning and he had a very good feeling about this meeting. He checked his watch for the time, and then called Gisela from the taxi. It was early afternoon in Paris and he knew she had plans to meet with a vendor after lunch at her boutique.

"Morning, my love, or afternoon I should say!"

She was thrilled to hear his voice. "Good morning, darling. How was your flight?"

"Uneventful, lonely. I miss you so much. How was the showing at the gallery?"

"It went well. Four oil paintings were sold, and a deposit was made on an abstract." Gisela was happy to stay in Paris a few days longer and help with the gallery event, and even prouder that it was a success.

"Great! Thanks, baby. I'm sorry I couldn't be there, but this is important for us, too."

"I totally agree. We're partners, remember?"

"Yes, we're partners." Christof smiled to himself. "Eternally, Mrs. Trist."

Gisela loved his passion, for her, for life, for everything. She looked at her watch. "Are you on your way to meet with the investors?"

"Not quite yet. I'm having breakfast with Nelson at 8:30 to go over the proposal. Then we're both meeting with the investors in his office at ten o'clock. Wish me luck. If it goes well, I can expand the New York gallery. We really need the space."

"Of course I wish you the best of luck. Give Mom and Dad a call when you can and let them know you're there. They're expecting to hear from you."

Silence fell briefly over the phone.

"Christof?"

"I'm here."

"You make me so happy."

"Baby, the connection is breaking up. I'll call you as soon as I'm out of the meeting. Love you."

"Love you too, bye."

Gisela paused for a moment, and then put the phone back to her ear.

"Christof?" This time he didn't answer her. He had turned off his phone and placed it in his jacket.

Gisela sighed as she missed telling him one last goodbye.

She hung up the phone and went back to her appointment. There was so much left to do, and the day was passing quickly. She had worked at the gallery filling in for Christof that morning, and then rushed to meet her vendor at La Boutique at one o'clock. His company's new line of fall handbags was selling quickly, and she had several reorders to place with him. After that, she hoped to help her assistant, Monique, rework the window displays before the shop closed at five-thirty.

When the taxi stopped, Christof Werner Trist checked his watch again. It was almost 8:30 and even with traffic, he had arrived right on time. He opened the door and stood, looking up at the tall skyline of the World Trade Center buildings. The sky was a calming shade of blue and perfectly clear. It was a beautiful September day in New York and he felt on top of the world.

CHAPTER EIGHT

Hours later, after constant efforts to connect to a telephone line out of the city, Gisela's frightened parents called from New York to see if she had heard from her husband. She remembered his breakfast meeting with Nelson at the World Trade Center. Before she could answer her father, he told her of the tragedy in New York... the country...She stayed and worked late at the boutique and hadn't heard...

She was standing in her bedroom, and in that moment, she felt her body fall weak and lifeless. She leaned back and slid slowly down the wall to the floor. There, Gisela sat, sobbing uncontrollably, and her parents felt helpless, so far way from their daughter. "Maybe it's not him, Gisela," her father said, trying to get her to talk to him. But she knew it was true, or she would have heard from him. He would have found a way to call her when it happened. She looked up at the clock, trying to convert Paris time to New York time. It had been hours since the first tower was hit.

Eventually, she did receive a call. This time, the call was from someone she didn't know, someone who seemed to be in emotional pain himself. His voice trembled as he spoke.

"I'm looking for the family of a Christof Werner Trist?"

"Yes." Gisela could barely speak.

"Are you Mrs. Trist?" The gentleman's voice cracked from exhaustion and grief.

"Yes."

"Mrs. Trist, I'm sorry to have to call and tell you this. Your husband's body has been…."

She moaned into the phone, "No, don't say it!" before he even had a chance to finish his sentence. She knew what she needed to know and she couldn't bear to hear what else he was about to say. Gisela hung up the phone and rolled over on the bed, once again pulling Christof's pillow back against her face to smell his fragrance and fill it with more tears.

Her heart and soul, like so many others that day, broke into a million painful pieces. Life for her would never be the same without her beloved Christof.

CHAPTER NINE

Gisela's days became blurred with agony and pain. Her parents did what they could to console her, but it was unbearable for them to watch their daughter grieve so deeply. When flights resumed out of New York, they flew to Paris and stayed with her for the first few weeks, making sure she took care of herself and encouraging her to continue with her life.

She couldn't bear to attend the memorials in New York. Getting on a plane seemed impossible to her now. With her parent's help, she managed to get up each day and dress. Most days, Katharina sat on the sofa, and Gisela laid her head on her mother's lap, not wanting to be awake. She couldn't wait to go back to bed at night and be alone with her dreams of Christof.

When it came time for them to return to New York, Katharina called Gisela's best friend, Maritza. They saw how Gisela seemed to feel better each time she received a call from her. Katharina asked if Maritza could come to Paris and visit Gisela, and she was happy to do so. Maritza arranged to fly to Paris and spend a month with Gisela. It was difficult, at first, to encourage Gisela to get out and do things. But with Maritza there, she soon began to take interest again in her boutique. By the third week, she even worked a few hours each day.

In addition to her own business concerns, decisions had to be made about Christof's galleries, and Maritza helped Gisela think through all of her options. She finally decided that she wanted to keep Christof's Paris gallery open, but it would be too difficult for her to manage the Frankfurt and New York locations. Those businesses would have to be sold.

Maritza was glad to see that her friend was making solid decisions again. In time, she felt Gisela would get through this. She was the strongest woman she knew. Maritza admired Gisela's determination to keep going on with her life after such a horrible tragedy. She would never have the strength to do this herself.

Before they knew it, the month was over. Gisela wanted Maritza to enjoy her last few days in Paris, so they shopped at Maritza's favorite stores and dined at some of the local's favorite restaurants. They talked and laughed together, and never ran out of things to say to each other. This time had brought them even closer together, and when Maritza was back home in New York, they continued to speak almost daily.

Months had passed since that horrible tragedy. On that particular day, Maritza had just returned from taking her husband, David, to the airport. She looked out of her apartment window at the first leaves on the trees. The winter had been milder than usual and the trees seemed anxious for spring to begin. She sat down on the window seat to sort through the mail and enjoy her afternoon tea. One envelope caught her attention and she opened it quickly, as it was a letter from her close friend, Gisela.

My dear friend Maritza,

Thank you so much for the journal. I plan to use it every day. You're always thinking of me and I do appreciate our friendship. I have had to make so many decisions about the galleries, and, although it is difficult, I am determined to continue Christof's projects. I hired an assistant, Nadia, to help with the closing in Frankfurt. I don't know what I would do without her. Unless, of course, you want to come back and work with me!

I am planning a trip to New York to meet with our investors, and to inventory the paintings that remain in the loft. They need to be distributed between Frankfurt and Paris. I'm bringing Nadia with me to help. While we're there, I want to take her to the summer house. I know its still off-season, but she's never seen the ocean, and she's been working so hard for me. I thought I'd treat her to a little vacation time while we're there. Would you like to join us for a quiet weekend away from the city?

I need time to clear my thoughts and take a break from the sadness I feel. Please try to come. Call me when you get this and we'll plan the details. Give my best to David.

Love, Gisela

Maritza's eyes welled with tears as she thought of Christof and Gisela, and how they loved each other so deeply. She and David once had passion and happiness, but nowhere near the bond of those two.

Maritza met David on a flight from London to New York eight years ago. She was the lead flight attendant that evening, and David was the captain of the Boeing 747. She had worked for the airlines for several years, but never flew with Captain David Lane. It was a whirlwind romance, and soon after their first overnight they were nearly inseparable. David was captivated by Maritza's beauty. She was a blonde with green eyes and a tanned, slim figure. He especially loved her remarkable zest for fun and adventure. She never thought she could feel so head over heels for any man. David had dark, almost exotic features, jet black hair and deep, soulfully dark eyes she could lose herself in, and looked amazing in and out of his uniform.

Each month, they planned their schedules so they could fly the same international trips and enjoy extended layovers together. David seemed devoted to his new love and lavished her with attention and gifts. By the end of their first year together, he had convinced her to marry him. By the end of the second year, she left her job with the airlines and settled in this New York apartment with him.

As time passed, her happiness made way for increasing loneliness, as the overseas routes expanded and his trips kept him away from home. She tried to stay busy, first by remodeling the entire apartment. She visited several galleries in search of art for their new home, and met Christof at a showing of his in Soho. She fell in love with his use of bold color, and soon purchased several pieces for their home. After buying the second piece, she received invitations to his showings and never missed seeing his new work.

One evening, both she and David attended a reception downtown and Maritza was happy to see that Christof had a beautiful woman at his side. It was Gisela, his new wife. She was stunningly beautiful and charming. This was the first showing she had attended as his wife, and the guests were fascinated with his lovely French bride. Christof introduced Mrs. Lane to Gisela, and Maritza was thrilled to find that Gisela lived in Paris, Maritza's favorite city. She had spent much of her time with the airlines flying between New York and Paris and loved to shop there during extended layovers.

Gisela, feeling the responsibility of staying close to her husband as he greeted the other guests, excused herself, but asked Maritza to meet her the next day for lunch. They agreed to meet at one o'clock at a small restaurant just down from the gallery.

David, having very little interest in attending the showing, had moved over by the bar, waiting for Maritza to leave. He too had noticed the beautiful Gisela and wondered what she and Maritza could possibly have in common.

When she finally found him at the bar, Maritza told him of her new acquaintance. "Remember the wonderful time we used to have on our Paris layovers? Well, Gisela lives in Paris! We're having lunch tomorrow. I can't wait to hear all about her life there!"

As usual, he ignored the conversation. He paid his bar tab and then walked outside to hail a taxi. When one finally pulled over and stopped for them, David darted into the taxi and she followed.

The following day, Maritza arrived at the restaurant and found Gisela already seated. By the time their first course had arrived, they had become deeply involved in conversation. They led such different lives, yet had much in common. They both loved fashion, travel, and everything about Paris. They even wore the same L'san fragrance, *Amour Mystérieux*.

From that luncheon meeting, their friendship grew and, in time, the two were the best of friends. Even with Gisela living in Paris, the distance between them never mattered. Each was just a phone call away from the other. Bored with her own home life, Maritza thrived on Gisela's stories of her life, her business, and her romantic journeys with Christof.

That was, of course, until Christof's death. Now, Gisela needed her more than ever. And Maritza never failed to support her best friend.

She laid the letter on the window seat and leaned back against the glass. She closed her eyes and thought about how awful it had been with David that morning.

He left early to go work out and returned home and showered. He packed his bag as she prepared an early lunch for the two of them. David was due at the airport at three-thirty, so she was hoping they had time to talk about vacation plans before he left on his Paris trip. This time he would be gone for five days.

David packed methodically, refusing to take more than one roller bag. When they were first married, Maritza used to sneak notes into his bag. They were mostly silly, missing you kinds of messages, but always with a drop of *Amour Mystérieux* perfume on the paper. As time passed, David complained to her that when he unpacked for his overnights, his uniforms smelled so feminine he was embarrassed to wear them, so she stopped writing love notes.

Maritza filled the water glasses and sat down to wait for David. Taking some time away from home was very important to her. She longed for Parisian nights with him. Those had been the best times of her life. Hopefully, she could convince him to take her with him on his next trip and they could rekindle the passion they once had. Where better than Paris to be together, away from it all? Maybe she could even sneak in a little time with Gisela.

David began to lose his temper as soon as he heard of her plans to join him. "Damn, Maritza! Why do you insist on smothering me?"

"Smothering you? What does that mean?"

David left the table and went into the bedroom. Maritza followed him, until he stopped and stood in front of the dresser mirror with his back to her. She continued to talk to him, watching him brush his hair and look at his reflection in the mirror. "I just thought we could spend some time together, David. Like we used to before I left my job. We could sightsee, take in a few clubs, and shop on the Champs-Élysées. You have almost four full days in the city. I want to be with you." Maritza came up closer behind him and put her arms around his waist. "I miss you, David."

David pulled away. "I don't want you there, okay?"

She began to get angry and cry. "You don't want me there? Why? Who is it now, David? Are you sleeping with someone else?"

David slammed the closet door and stared back at her. "What are you fucking talking about, Maritza?"

She saw how angry she had made him. As David finished dressing, she pleaded with him to forgive her. "I'm sorry. I'm just tired of being alone."

"Well, I'm fucking sick of your whining. You wanted this apartment, so I got it for you. You bought out every store on Fifth Avenue to furnish it, and I never complained. Clothes, shoes, and jewelry...those expensive paintings! I've given you everything you want. Why can't you just be happy?"

He zipped his roller bag and took one more look at himself in the mirror. "Are you taking me, or am I calling for a ride?"

She picked up her jacket and handbag and followed him downstairs to the garage. When he reached their car, he opened the trunk and put his roller bag in first, and then his flight bag. Next, he carefully laid his jacket and hat over them so they wouldn't get wrinkled or crushed. Then he opened the passenger door, but not for her. He slid into the seat and motioned for her to drive.

They remained silent on the way to the airport. She was annoyed that he never buckled his seatbelt when he wore his uniform. He said it ruined a starched shirt. But she didn't say anything to him about the safety issue, because that would start another argument.

David looked at his watch occasionally and glanced over to see how fast she was driving, but never said a word. All he could think about was how screwed up his life would be if he brought her to Paris on one of his flights. It was hard enough dealing with her little vacation to see Gisela last fall. He had to cancel one of his trips that month to avoid running into her.

As they pulled up to the departure level, David got out of the car and stood, waiting for her to release the trunk. He put on his jacket, and then placed his bags on the curb. He walked around to the driver's window and knocked on the glass. Maritza lowered the window.

"I'm going to be back in a few days. We'll talk about it then, okay?"

Maritza looked up at him; all she could see was her reflection in his black aviator glasses. She hated the fact that he looked so handsome in his uniform. "All right, we'll talk then."

He could tell from her voice he needed to do a little damage control. He lowered his sunglasses so she could see his eyes. "Do you love me? Maritza, look at me. *Do you love me?*"

"Yes, maybe too much."

He leaned over and kissed her on the cheek. "I'll call you when I get in." With that, he walked around the car and gathered his things. She watched him put on his hat before walking into the terminal. He used to turn and wave goodbye to her before he walked through the glass doors, but he had stopped doing that a long time ago.

She drove home feeling lonely and emotionally drained. She felt she had nothing to look forward to until, when she arrived home, she found that she had this letter from Paris.

Maritza read Gisela's note again and wiped her tears away. She tried to call her, first in Paris and then in Frankfurt, but realized it was the wrong hour to call. She left a message that she received her letter and would love to go away with her for a few days.

She picked up the mail, straightened up the living room, and managed to clear the dishes from lunch, leaving them in the sink to wash another time. She went into the bedroom, which still smelled of David's aftershave. After a hot shower, Maritza put on David's robe and settled down to read, but she was exhausted from the day and soon fell asleep.

She welcomed it, because sleep helped her to escape from her troubles. In fact, it was her little secret. Sometimes she would sleep off and on for days when David was traveling, having little desire to get out of the apartment, or to even get dressed. When it was time to go to the airport to pick him up from his trip, she would have everything perfectly clean, leaving no evidence of the empty life she led when he was away from her.

CHAPTER TEN

It was mealtime for the cockpit crew. Since 9/11, the procedure to deliver the meals now involved several crewmembers. Lisette was the lead flight attendant, and she called the crew to advise them of the meal selection. It was Trans-Global's policy that pilots were not served the same meals in order to prevent a possible food reaction, so it was David who made the first selection. First Officer Wabash, whom David nicknamed *Cannonball*, would be served a different entrée. The relief pilot would choose from the remaining meal selections.

Marc, a flight attendant who was working in first class, prepared the trays and Lisette notified the other two first class attendants that they were to prepare for cockpit entry. As they positioned the beverage carts in the cabin entry from the galley, Marc stood at the cockpit door as Lisette called to notify Captain Lane that the area was secure and requested meal delivery to the cockpit.

Cannonball confirmed visually through the security viewer on the door that it was the meal service. Captain Lane nodded for the door to be unlocked. As Lisette entered the cockpit, Cannonball reached around her tiny waist and latched the door.

Lisette served the trays and chatted briefly with the crew. "What, no beans and cornbread tonight, Lisette?" Cannonball spoke with his long southern drawl. She couldn't help but laugh when she was around him. He loved to tease her, asking for catsup and sweet tea with his meals. His food preferences were quite foreign to this Parisian city girl. "Lisette, you don't know what real livin' is until you sit down for a meal of beans, taters, cornbread, and sweet tea."

"I'll take your word for it," she said as she smiled at him.

David asked her how things were going in the cabin.

"Just fine, Captain."

"Good. Looking ahead on radar, we should have a smooth ride. Once you're back in the cabin, we'll go ahead and turn off the seatbelt sign."

"Got it. Is there anything else I can get for you gentlemen?"

"No, we're fine."

"Okay then. Let me know when you're ready for the trays to be collected."

Cannonball contacted Marc to confirm the area was still secure, and then opened the door for Lisette to exit the cockpit, locking it behind her. Once the cabin crew saw that the cockpit was no longer vulnerable, they completed the after-dinner beverage service, dimmed the cabin lights, and prepared for what they hoped to be a quiet flight for the next few hours.

After the galleys were cleared, Lisette and Marc sat in their seats and relaxed for a few minutes while the other flight attendants monitored the cabin. Lisette and Marc both lived in Paris and frequently bid for this Paris/New York trip.

It had been a smooth ride to Charles De Gaulle, and even with de-icing and two ground holds, they managed to get into Paris on time. It was eleven a.m. before they arrived at the hotel, and in the taxi the crew had been discussing how they planned to spend the day. Four of the flight attendants and one of the pilots lived in Paris, so they had already headed home from the airport.

The remaining crew all agreed that they would change when they checked in and meet in the lobby around noon for lunch, except David, who said he was tired and wanted to catch up on some sleep. They were used to him going about on his own. In fact, the regulars who frequently flew with Captain Lane referred to him as a "slam-clicker," slang the airline had for crewmembers that reached their hotel room, closed the door, and clicked the lock. They were rarely seen again in the hotel until it was time to report for the next trip.

Once checked in, David went up the elevator to his room. Whenever he stayed in a hotel for an overnight, one of the first things he did was to open a window. After years of traveling in and out of time zones, he had learned to perfect his sleep ritual and rest, and the fresh air helped him to relax. Even in the winter, he continued to let the fresh air in, which made the room uncomfortably cold in the morning, but perfect for sleeping.

That week's trip had brought him to Paris for a four-day overnight, and he had looked forward to his stay at the Hotel Parc. The hotel was located on Avenue Rapp, just a short walk away from the Eiffel Tower. Although David rarely visited the tourist areas, his favorite room overlooked a side street, with French doors opening up to a spectacular view of the Eiffel Tower. He usually called ahead to request this corner room, and the hotel manager was always accommodating. In fact, after so many requests from crewmembers, this corner room and the sixteen additional rooms on the same floor were blocked solely for Trans-Global crewmembers, executives, and their families. The hotel manager was happy to provide the airline with these better rooms because they guaranteed him full-floor occupancy year-round at a premium rate.

But this time, David changed clothes quickly and took a taxi to the Champs-Élysées. No matter how often he visited Paris, he was always impressed with the stores. Today, he planned to shop at his favorite accessory boutique, *Lacet Rose*.

Simone helped him to select a beautiful silk scarf from their latest collection. He watched as she wrapped it in their white lace signature box and tied it firmly with red grosgrain ribbon. "Your wife, she will love this! How is Madame Lane?" She remembered when he and Maritza would come into the shop. David smiled at her and answered, "She's well, thank you." Simone smiled back and thanked him for his business.

With the sale completed, she, along with the other women in the store, admired his good looks as he walked out the door. Simone, rarely impressed with American tourists, found this couple fascinating. He was so handsome and flirtatious, and his wife was such a contrast to his dark looks, so feminine with long blonde hair and gorgeous green eyes. The last time she had seen Maritza was when she and Gisela shopped there last fall. Simone had asked Maritza how she liked the peach and cream silk scarf, and Maritza seemed puzzled by her question. So Simone apologized and said she must have been thinking of another customer. *Not so, though. Could her happily married, handsome American customer be making purchases for another love interest?*

David walked to the local *chocolatier* and chose a box of their best truffles. After hailing a taxi, he returned to the hotel, retrieved his room key from the desk clerk, and headed to his room.

Later that evening, he slipped on his robe and stood by the open French doors. The only light coming into the room was from a café's flashing sign, which was located across the street. He sipped the last drop of champagne from his glass and settled into bed.

David slept soundly until his pager began to vibrate on the bedside table. He looked at the clock: three a.m. Crew scheduling, no doubt, with a change in report time.

He rolled over to get a few hours more sleep before he called to deal with whatever they had for him. He was guaranteed minimum rest, and he needed the sleep.

Minutes later, his cell phone rang. David, while fumbling for his phone, knocked the gold candy box off the bedside table and the last truffle rolled across the rug.

"David?"

"Yeah. Why are you calling in the middle of the night? What's wrong?"

"Nothing's wrong."

"C'mon, Maritza, it's fucking three in the morning here."

"Sorry, David. I lost track of the time. Remember our overnights in Paris? We were hardly in bed by five, partying all night and sleeping during the day. I was feeling lonely and wanted to hear your voice. I'm really sorry I woke you."

"You know how I am about getting my rest."

"Sorry, I'll hang up now. I love you."

"Me, too. Bye."

David rolled over and noticed a light coming from the bathroom. Soon, the light went out, the room was dark again, and he helped Lisette settle back in close to him. When the phone rang and she realized it was his wife, she had gone into the bathroom. It was hard to hear him talk to her, even harder to hear him tell her he loved her.

"Sorry, baby." Lisette kissed him passionately, told him goodnight, and melted into his arms. She smiled as she felt his body respond to her warmth, and soon his hands were exploring her breasts and between her legs. Before long they were making love again, satisfying each other's needs, and then they both drifted back off to sleep.

David woke early, showered, and dressed. He stood by the French doors, watching a street vendor set up for the day's business. He couldn't get Maritza off his mind. *She never called him during the night.* Her call left him unsettled. *Does she know?*

Lisette slid out of bed and came up behind him, putting her arms around his waist. "What's wrong?"

"I have things I have to do today, thought I'd get an early start." David turned around and kissed her on the neck, and then picked up his wallet and room key.

Lisette was familiar with this tone of his voice. It was the phone call that made him so distant.

"I'll be gone all day. Call you tonight." David winked at her and walked out of the door.

Lisette wrapped his robe around her and walked out onto the balcony. She saw David leave the hotel and hail a taxi. She showered, repacked her bag, and left him this note before leaving to go home:

> *Bonjour, Monsieur Captain!*
> *So good of you to meet me in Paris!*
> *I will be awaiting your call tonight.*
> *Dinner at eight, Le Bistro Royale?*
> *Oui? Mademoiselle Lisette*

Downstairs in the hotel atrium, several crewmembers were enjoying morning coffee and breakfast. When the elevator door opened, Lisette entered the lobby. One of the flight attendants noticed her. "Lisette! Hi, come and join us." The others stared as she continued to walk toward the door to leave. "What's up with that? She just ignored us."

The other flight attendants stared at each other until one finally spoke, "She *lives* in Paris; she's based here." They began to speculate why she would be at the hotel in the morning with her bags.

Cannonball looked out the window and watched her get into a taxi. He had no doubt why she was there at the hotel. *David, old buddy, you and I are going to have a talk.*

After everyone finished breakfast, they left together to do some sightseeing. Cannonball excused himself and said he'd catch up with them later at the Louvre. First, he was going back to his room to call his wife.

CHAPTER ELEVEN

Madame Trist was unusually quiet today, and Nadia noticed the change in her personality.

"Nadia..."

"Yes, Madame?"

"Come and take a break with me and enjoy some tea."

Nadia came into her office and found Madame Trist sitting at her conference table. "Come, sit down and join me."

Nadia sat down with her, placing the napkin across her lap. The tea was already made and her cup poured. She added a dab of milk and waited to hear what Madame Trist had on her mind.

"Nadia, I spoke with Mrs. Schiller early this morning. She called to tell me that you're conflicted between your job and your engagement. Naturally, I believe your family comes before your job, and I don't want you to be in an awkward position. I would certainly understand if you needed to take some time for yourself. Wedding preparation can be very time consuming."

Nadia suddenly felt her heart begin to race. "Madame Trist, I want to work. I plan to continue working for you until you close the gallery. After that, I hope to find another job. I need money for school, for a wedding...Nicolas and I are a long way from me staying home to raise a family. I hope you believe that."

"I do believe you, Nadia. I just want you to feel you have a choice whether or not to stay."

"Thank you, Madame." Nadia seemed composed on the outside, but inside she was fuming! *How dare Hula call Madame Trist and interfere with her job!* "She's just trying to make life difficult for us. She had no right to call you."

"Actually, I met with her last night. She was my evening appointment. She came in to see the watercolors, and then called me this morning to express her concerns that this job might create difficulty between you and her son."

Tears began to sting Nadia's eyes.

"I know that under the circumstances, with Christof's death, it might be more difficult for you to come and tell me that you need time for you and your fiancé. Of course I would understand. I only want the best for you."

"Madame Trist, my future mother-in-law may have called you to see a painting, but what she was really interested in was to make you question my loyalty. You don't know her. She doesn't like me. She definitely doesn't want me to marry her son."

"Well, then. You have your hands full, my dear. Are you sure you want to deal with such a meddling mother-in-law?"

"Nicolas and I will take care of Hula. She won't be contacting you again."

Gisela smiled at Nadia. *She's so young to have such worries*, she thought. "Then let's forget it all happened, and plan our trip to the States." She handed Nadia an envelope. "Inside are your plane ticket and itinerary. I thought you might want to give a copy to your parents."

Nadia opened the envelope and saw her first plane ticket. She couldn't wait to show Mama and Papa. Looking over the itinerary, she saw the travel dates were earlier than expected.

"I thought we were going in May."

"We are, but I also need to make a quick trip now to take care of a few things, see my family, and Maritza. I thought you might want to join me."

Nadia was thrilled. "There's no hotel listed on the itinerary. Where will we be staying in New York?"

"We'll be staying in my husband's…Christof's loft."

Nadia saw the sadness in her eyes when she paused to speak her husband's name. She was surprised that they were going to stay there. As far as she knew, Madame Trist hadn't been back to the loft since he died.

"Nadia, I appreciate you being with me. I haven't even flown since…"

"Oh, you don't have to thank me! I'm thrilled to be going with you!" Nadia finished her tea and offered to pour Madame Trist another cup.

As she cleared the dishes, Madame Trist opened her briefcase and continued her work.

Nadia looked at the clock. *Nicolas should be at work by now.* Even with the excitement of the trip, she was still upset over Hula's interference. She sat down at her desk and dialed the bank number. It was still too early for the bank to be open, but Nicolas decided to answer the phone.

"She what? Nadia, are you sure? Maybe Madame Trist thought she meant something she didn't. I mean, you know my mother. Sometimes she insinuates something without actually coming out and saying it." There was silence on the other end of the phone, so Nicolas decided he better stop trying to explain his mother's actions. He could tell that Nadia was getting more upset.

"I'll call her now and straighten this whole thing out. Don't worry, honey, she won't be interfering with your job again."

Nadia saw that her other line was ringing so she couldn't keep him on the phone for long. "I love you, Nicolas. Please do something about this."

"I love you, too. I'll call you tonight."

Madame Trist couldn't help overhearing the conversation. "Nadia, what do you say we both get our work done and leave a little early today?"

Nadia was glad, because she had an extra stop to make on the way home.

CHAPTER TWELVE

Hula and Oskar rarely spoke in the mornings, but today Hula was unusually cheerful. Oskar dreaded coming downstairs. He knew that breakfast would be a guessing game, with Hula's mood driving the conversation.

Hula called upstairs for her husband to join her for breakfast. Oskar looked into the mirror at his tired face and straightened his tie. He gathered his wallet and pocket watch and headed down the stairs.

On the table were eggs, würst, hot potatoes, brötchen, and his favorite—spiced apple butter. Hula hummed an unfamiliar tune as she poured her husband a cup of hot coffee. "Good morning, Oskar. Did you sleep well?"

Oskar was puzzled by her graciousness. She rarely offered him such a fine morning meal. Still feeling uneasy from last night's heavy drinking, Oskar pushed the plate away and focused on his coffee. "I slept alright."

"It's a wonder, Oskar. You didn't come to bed until after two in the morning. How can you expect to work without any rest?"

If he didn't know better, he thought she almost sounded concerned. When he stayed in his study late at night drinking, it usually resulted in an early morning argument. He knew she was up to something. Otherwise, she would have greeted him with an icy stare.

"Oskar?"

"What?"

"Oh, never mind."

Hula and Oskar were sitting quietly, drinking coffee until the phone rang. Hula got up to answer the call.

"Mother!"

"Nicolas, what's wrong?"

"I just received a call from Nadia, Mother. She's very upset."

"Oh?"

"Why did you speak with Madame Trist? It seems that she's filled with questions now about Nadia's commitment to her job because of a conversation she had with you."

"Son, I simply called Madame Trist to make an appointment to see a painting that she has on sale. She mentioned that she would not be able to show the piece, but her assistant would be available. Naturally, I informed her of our acquaintance with Nadia."

"*Acquaintance?* She's your future daughter-in-law, Mother! Besides, that's not the issue. Why does she think Nadia shouldn't be working for her?"

"I never said that, darling. Madame Trist must have misunderstood me."

"Nadia loves her job and plans to continue working, Mother. I want her to enjoy her life, and if that means she wants to work outside of the home, then I support her completely."

"Well, that's very good of you, Nicolas."

Hearing the conversation from the kitchen, Oskar shook his head. He stood up, reached for the whiskey decanter, and poured a shot into his coffee. *So that explains her good mood this morning. She's happy because she found a way to make the engaged couple miserable.*

Oskar hurried to finish his coffee and head out the back door before she hung up the phone.

After lunch, Nadia asked Madame Trist if she could leave for the day. Her work was caught up and there were no appointments coming in. She hurried to make the afternoon train home. Upon arriving at her stop, this time she walked toward the Schillers' home. She knocked on the door and waited for Hula to answer. As she was preparing to knock again, the door opened.

Hula was startled to see Nadia, but kept her composure as she invited her to come in.

"Well, this is a surprise. How nice to see you. Won't you sit down?"

"Actually, I think I'll stand, thank you. Mrs. Schiller, I understand you called Madame Trist this morning, and you also came to the gallery last night."

"Well, yes, I did."

"May I ask why?"

"Certainly, dear. I found an advertisement for the Trist Gallery and I was interested in seeing some paintings. You know, the paintings in the bank could be upgraded. They've been hanging there for years."

"Is that the only reason you contacted her?"

"Why, yes."

"Then why did you find it necessary to discuss *my job* with Madame Trist?"

"I don't know what you mean. Why would I discuss your work with her? She mentioned that her assistant could show me the paintings, and I told her we knew each other. What's wrong with that, dear?"

Nadia turned and walked toward the door.

"Leaving so soon?"

"I have to go, Mrs. Schiller. And by the way, we don't advertise the gallery locally."

Nadia walked out and Hula closed the door.

Hula leaned back against the door and smiled. *That little trip to Frankfurt proved to be worthwhile. I didn't expect Madame Trist to work so quickly with the hints I dropped about Nadia's work. Little Nadia will never marry my Nicolas. He deserves so much more. I'll find a way to save him from a life with that little nobody.*

When Nadia arrived home, it was mid-afternoon and Mama was out shopping. She was glad to be alone. She went to her room and called Nicolas, but he was with a client. She didn't leave a message. She lay back on her bed and closed her eyes. Her head hurt from the day's tension. Soon, she was asleep.

Mama peeked in on her when Nicolas stopped by a few hours later, and she was fast asleep. He decided she must really be tired and asked Mama not to wake her. He stayed and visited for a while with Isabella and George, and enjoyed a slice of Isabella's delicious Black Forest Cake.

Before heading home, Nicolas asked Isabella for a piece of paper. He wrote a note to Nadia that he had come by to see her, but she was asleep and he didn't want to wake her. He told her that he loved her, and not to worry about anything. He would always be there to take care of her.

When Mama went to bed that evening, she covered Nadia with the quilt she made for her when she was a little girl, and left Nicolas's note on her nightstand.

Papa came into Nadia's room and Mama stepped out into the hallway to wait for him. He kissed Nadia on the forehead and then turned out the light.

CHAPTER THIRTEEN

David had been home a few days from Paris and had also flown another quick trip to London. Maritza complained that he hadn't taken her out on the town for weeks, so when she mentioned her plans to be downtown for an appointment Thursday, he agreed to meet her for dinner that evening. He even let her choose the restaurant.

David sat at the bar and waited for her to arrive. She was late, as usual. He never liked coming here. Piano bars were never his thing. Not even the most famous piano bar in New York could keep his attention for long. But this cocktail waitress, now, was another thing. He struck up a conversation with the tall leggy brunette and managed to get her phone number before he finished his second drink.

Maritza finally arrived and looked inside the bar to see if David was still there. She was afraid that her tardiness would trigger him to storm off and leave without her. There he was, smiling and flirting with the girl behind the bar. Maritza felt a twinge of jealousy, seeing him have fun with another woman, but she decided to act as though she hadn't seen a thing. After checking her coat, she walked up behind him and put her hand on his shoulder.

David turned around and saw it was his wife. "Well, it's about time you got here. Where were you?"

"I was caught in traffic." Maritza looked at his bourbon, served neat as usual. "Started without me?"

"What was I fucking supposed to do here until you bothered to show up?" David downed his bourbon, winked at the bartender, and left cash for her on the bar. "C'mon, let's go eat."

They had reservations for dinner and their favorite maitre d' was at the podium. "Mr. and Mrs. Lane, how good to see you again. Right this way." At least this part of the evening was going well. The table he had for them was on the terrace, and the white twinkling lights made for a romantic setting.

Maritza wanted to talk to David about returning to work, but she could see he was in a mood. She decided to keep her decision to herself for a while. Hopefully, by the end of the meal he would be more relaxed and she could approach him about her idea to return to her job at the airlines.

David ordered a steak and another bourbon. Maritza couldn't decide what to eat, which annoyed him. After ordering an avocado, mandarin orange, and goat cheese salad and chardonnay, she tried to exchange small talk to get the bartender off of her mind, and off of his.

"Your sister called today."

David looked at her and then went back to his bourbon.

"David, I *said* Jana called."

He was annoyed that she insisted he speak. "Okay, *what* did she have to say?"

"Jana wants to know when we're coming to visit her in California."

"You know what to tell her."

"I did, but she's *your* sister, David. I'm tired of putting her off this way."

"I don't have time to go to see her, you know that."

"Do I know that, David? Why can't you take some time off and go to San Francisco? You haven't even seen your nephew and he's almost two. Your parents aren't getting any younger, either."

"C'mon, Maritza. If you want to go to California, use your flight benefits and go. But get off my back, will you?"

"Get off your back?" She had planned to let the little bar scene go, but she didn't like the tone he had just taken with her. "By the way, don't you think you were acting a little too familiar with the brunette in the bar?"

This made him angry and this time he spoke loudly. "Why is it that you're always accusing me of trying to get into bed with every woman I meet?"

She realized that she needed to calm things down, so she leaned toward him and spoke softly. "I'm not accusing you of anything, David. Just let it go. I'm sorry I mentioned it."

They sat for what seemed forever in silence. Finally, the meal arrived and they spoke briefly with the wait staff. David continued to order bourbon throughout the meal, and Maritza tried to keep her emotions together. She had asked him to make these reservations for dinner because she missed those great evenings they once had. The excitement of meeting at the bar, then dinner, dancing...romance. The chase. That's what she missed the most.

He was such a romantic man before they were married. He lavished her with bottles of her favorite pouilly-fuisse wine and chocolates. Sheets covered with rose petals and beautiful gifts. Having spent so much of their time working together for the airlines, they both had the seniority to bid for the same trips. Days lounging in Paris, London, and Madrid now seemed like a dream that had never happened.

Most importantly, he knew how to get her in bed and how to keep her coming back to him. And that was precisely what made her afraid today, and her desire to return to the airlines was for more than one reason. She needed to keep an eye on him. Up close and personal.

She wanted to order dessert, but David frowned at her. "You need to watch what you're eating, Maritza. You're gaining weight. Don't do that to me." She passed on the dessert tray and ordered black coffee.

"David, I need to discuss something with you. "

He looked up at her. "What?"

"I called and spoke with Martina today."

"Martina? Martina who?"

"My friend Martina, in human resources at Trans-Global. They've lifted their hiring freeze for international flight attendants. I'm going back to work."

"What? I thought we settled this when we were married. You stay home and I work. Period."

"But, I thought it would..."

"No!" David knew he better get it together fast. He laid his hand on the white linen cloth and touched Maritza's hand. This time he lowered his voice and leaned in closer. "I mean, I thought you were happy to be out of that rat race."

"I'm happy, David, but I want us to spend more time together. Remember how wonderful it was when we both worked for Trans-Global? Now I only see you when you come home to empty your flight bag and fill it up again."

David's mind raced, looking for the right thing to say. *If I don't take care of this right now, it'll become a real problem.*

David looked into her green eyes for the first time this evening, "I'm sorry. I haven't been a very good husband lately."

"No, David, it's not that. I..."

"Look, forget about the airline thing. I'll move my trips around so I have more time at home. Maybe we can even take a trip to see Jana, or go on a real vacation. Isn't that what we really need to do, baby?"

Maritza looked at David and saw the guy she fell in love with. *Maybe if he would just fly less and spend more time with me I would feel closer to him. After all, if he were involved with someone, he certainly wouldn't be willing to give up flight time. That was his license to cheat without me knowing.*

"If you really think you can do that, David, it would be great. I just want us to spend more time together, like we used to. I miss you and even more important than that, I miss us."

David motioned for the check. Once that was done, he led Maritza into the bar. He ordered a bottle of their best pouilly-fuisse wine and took a corner table. For the next hour and a half, he poured her wine and whispered in her ear how much he loved and needed her. They danced to the piano tunes and he was perfect in her eyes again.

When their taxi arrived back at the apartment, he led her into the bedroom and made love to her until he could feel she was his again.

As she fell asleep dreaming of their wonderful life ahead, he stepped into the shower and tried to wash away this fucked up night. Whatever got into her head, he felt assured he had ended the discussion.

CHAPTER FOURTEEN

The next morning, David packed for his trip and Maritza seemed happy and satisfied after their night together. He encouraged her to sleep in so he could get ready in peace. Once she was dressed, she drove him to the airport and went on with her day. She was meeting her mother and they were going shopping.

When David cleared security and reached his departure gate, he took out his cell phone and called Edmond, the hotel concierge in Paris, and made arrangements for a chilled bottle of pouilly-fuisse wine to be placed in his room. It had been three weeks since he had seen Lisette, and he wanted to make sure that everything went as planned. *Those fucking flight attendants almost ruined a good thing for me the last time she left the hotel. Thank God it was Cannonball who flew that trip with me.* Cannonball had done David a favor and put an end to the gossip that started when the flight attendant recognized Lisette in the lobby.

Naturally, Cannonball had warned David to keep away from Lisette, but it would take more than a little gossip to keep him from his overnight activities. Cannonball had seen him through a few affairs over the years, but they were usually brief encounters with "newbies" (a newly trained flight attendant). It was easy to bed a few out of each new class, unless a more seasoned flight attendant looked out for them. He always got a kick out of a newbie calling him "Captain" in bed. Most of the newbies came to the airlines to find a husband, so they didn't last long anyway. The older ones packed travel bags with food and "slam-clicked" at the end of each day, and you never saw them until the next report time.

David couldn't believe that his friend never took advantage of the opportunity. He'd see him in the bar having a few drinks with the crew, but he always left alone to go to his room. David teased Cannonball that he wouldn't have sex with a flight attendant on an overnight even if she knocked on his hotel door and begged him for it.

"David, my buddy, I don't need the drama. Besides, I love my wife. She's more than I can handle," he told him. *And he meant it.*

The flight was uneventful and long. David didn't particularly care for either of the pilots scheduled to fly with him today. He missed Cannonball, who was taking a vacation with his family in Hawaii.

When the shuttle arrived at the hotel, he left his luggage in the lobby and took a moment to walk around the corner for a bouquet of flowers. *Corny,* he thought, *but she'll like it.*

Back at the hotel lobby, he handed Edmond cash for his trouble. The concierge hadn't minded waiting after his shift for David to arrive. Edmond not only admired David, he looked forward to his visits to Paris. He studied David: his dress, his mannerisms, how his grin affected the women he came in contact with, including the hotel staff. He imagined what it would be like to travel like him and have so many women want his attention.

He showered quickly, wrapped a towel around his waist, and sat on the bed to call her.

"Lisette, I'm here."

"Oh, David, I don't know about this. What if someone sees me?"

"I'm here. C'mon. Don't let me down."

Lisette finally agreed and told him she was on her way.

David's next call was to Maritza. "Hey, I just got to the hotel."

Maritza sighed. "You sound like you're exhausted."

"Yeah, this time change still kicks me. Anything going on?"

"Just lunch tomorrow with Katharina Sommer. I promised Gisela I would take her mom to lunch. Katharina worries so much about her, trying to close the galleries and all."

"Okay. Listen, I have to go."

"Love you, David."

"Me, too. Goodnight."

"Bye."

David hung up the phone and was glad that was over. He hated making those token calls home every day.

He leaned back on the bed and closed his eyes. Almost two hours passed before a knock on the door awoke him from a sound sleep.

He quickly wrapped the towel around his waist again and opened the door. Lisette smiled nervously at first and began to speak, but David quickly put his finger to her lips to quiet her and pulled her close to him. He looked deeply into her eyes and kissed her passionately. Tonight there would be no words spoken. He knew this would make her want him even more. He had choreographed this moment, and he could feel it working.

As they shared the wine, he kissed her neck and shoulders, undressing her ever so slowly, feeling her body relax with his soft touch. When he felt the urge, he took her. Gently, lovingly, so *unlike* him. But he had to be gentle with her, bringing her back into his web, removing her doubt and keeping her where he wanted her to be.

In this bed, on his timetable, whenever he wanted her. Paris overnights. No more, no less.

CHAPTER FIFTEEN

Almost daily, Maritza struggled with her life. When David was home, each day was difficult for her. If she approached him to ask a question, she risked the chance of being confronted with his temper. She rarely spoke to him about any controversial subject, particularly household issues. Having to deal with the everyday routine of a household drove him mad, so she rarely discussed home or family with him.

Consequently, his extended periods away left very little for them to share or talk about. She searched for common ground with him. His life was centered on flying, and she saw how happy his job made him. When asked by others if he liked his career, he would always respond, "There's no better office than upstairs."

Above all, Maritza struggled with her desire to be with him. She loved David and wanted him to be home with her, but his ego and attitude made him difficult to cope with at times. Although she yearned to be with him, she also dreaded him coming off a trip. She called the first day or two the bumpy re-entry period because it seemed to always bring turbulence. They argued over minor things, and he slept more than she thought he needed to, explained away by him as his need to adjust to the change in time zones.

She worked hard to have everything perfect at home, but inevitably he would find something to point out to her. She refrained from doing housework when he was home. He was a procedural person, which was a positive attribute to list on a pilot's resume, but when it came to their home, it created undue stress on Maritza. He took every opportunity to tell her the proper procedure to do anything and everything, from cooking to cleaning to dressing herself. Once, they had a tremendous fight over whether a woman should buckle her belt left to right, or right to left.

In general, most pilots she knew from her work at Trans-Global hated change in their surroundings, possibly from their need to have constant stability in the cockpit. He struggled with her need to redecorate, but it kept her busy and quiet, so he tried to deal with it.

Over time, her confidence level waned and she began to question herself on the simplest of decisions. David noticed the changes in his wife and felt as though she was becoming a weak person, and he had no tolerance of that behavior in anyone. Some days, she found it hard to get out of bed in the morning. She hated the fact that he seemed on top of the world that she felt was falling to pieces around her.

Maritza carried another secret that she never revealed to anyone. Not to David, not to Gisela, not to her family. Her doctor had prescribed a number of antidepressants over the past three years, and nothing seemed to work for any length of time. Within a few months of starting each one, she would have a "breakthrough," her doctor called them, and he would either increase her dosage or change her to an entirely different drug.

She had trouble sleeping, then slept too much. Her head buzzed as she went on and off each medication, and she hated the feeling it gave her. But her family doctor convinced her it would help with what he diagnosed as panic attacks, so she kept trying the pills he prescribed.

The attacks didn't start until she left the airlines. The first time she knew something was terribly wrong was when she was standing at a jewelry counter shopping downtown with David. He was looking at an aviation watch, playfully flirting with the salesgirl. Maritza stood near him.

At first, she was looking at the watch selection in the adjoining case. In the next few seconds, she felt a sinking feeling. David and the salesgirl continued to talk and joke back and forth and, although Maritza could still hear their voices, her focus moved inward. *Was she going to faint? Was it a heart attack causing her heart to beat out of her chest?* The lights in the store seemed to dim. She felt an urge to run, even though dizziness had caused her to lean against the counter. *Would she die right here by the escalator?* Although it seemed like an eternity, within a minute or so, the feeling began to pass. In fact, David never noticed that she was in trouble. He made his selection and purchased the multi-dial watch. Then, he turned to her to say he was going for a cup of coffee.

Maritza tried to compose herself and continue with him to the coffee shop, but the episode left her feeling weak and unsettled. She made the excuse that she was tired and it irritated him, as he was in town for only one more day and needed to pick up a few things. She told him to go finish his shopping without her. She sat in the coffee shop, trying to grasp what had just happened. When she felt she could make it home okay, she hailed a taxi.

She changed into her robe and made herself a pot of hot tea. She needed to do something normal to help her forget that crazy, awful feeling of not being in control. She tried to clear her mind and start a new novel she had picked up that morning, but her thoughts kept drifting back to those frightening moments at the department store.

CHAPTER SIXTEEN

Maritza never told anyone about her episode at the department store. A few uneventful weeks passed by, so she decided it must have been caused by a drop in her blood sugar. Now, she was careful to eat small meals more frequently throughout the day and keep herself hydrated.

One morning, she was meeting her mother for a book signing at their favorite bookstore. When she stepped out of the taxi and walked into the store, she froze. The same feeling came over her, but this time Bettina had arrived early and was watching for her daughter. She saw her become pale and disoriented. Bettina rushed over and took Maritza's hand and led her to a seating area. By the time Maritza sat down, she was in tears.

"Something's wrong, Mom. I'm freaking out. I have to get out of here."

"Not just yet, darling." Bettina reached into her bag for her cell phone.

"Who are you calling, Mom?" Maritza laid her head back and her eyes welled with tears. *Oh my God, it's happening again. What could possibly be wrong with me?*

Bettina arranged to take her daughter to see Dr. Hammond Cox. He had been their physician for years and was a close family friend. Bettina spoke with him directly and he told her to bring her right in. He would be waiting for them.

After a complete exam, he encouraged her to go home and take it easy. She returned three days later for her lab results.

"I'm not pregnant, am I?"

"No, Maritza. You're not pregnant. Why? Were you hoping for that?"

"Not at all. David and I agreed not to have any children. At least not for a few years, anyway."

She lied, hoping these episodes meant that she was pregnant. *Maybe that would make David interested in me again.*

"All of your lab work came out perfect, Maritza. In fact, you're the specimen of physical health."

Maritza breathed a sigh of relief. "Then what could cause those feelings I've been having, Dr. Cox?"

"I think we need to take a look at some emotional issues. How have you been lately...are you and David getting along well?"

"Of course we are! What does that have to do with anything? Did Mom say something to you?"

"I'm just getting some background, Maritza. Emotional stress, our environment...they're all important in diagnosing..."

Maritza began to cry. Dr. Cox reached over for the box of tissues and laid them on the table.

"Maritza, I've known you for a long time. Is there something you're not telling me?"

"Yes." She decided to tell him of her first episode in the department store and how it had frightened her, just like it did when she went to meet her mother. Dr. Cox listened intently and Maritza was relieved to speak openly about her fear of losing control.

After a few more questions, Dr. Cox diagnosed her experiences as panic attacks. He explained the theory of "fight or flight," which most patients describe as their overwhelming desire to run from the environment they're in when the attack begins.

He gave her samples of an antidepressant that he wanted her to try. She resisted. "I'm not depressed, Dr. Cox." He explained that antidepressants were used successfully to treat panic attack disorder along with multiple other disorders, such as compulsiveness. He told her that a drug must be approved by the FDA for a specific purpose, but can actually produce successful results in treating a variety of other ailments.

She decided to give them a try for thirty days, although Dr. Cox told her it could take several weeks for her to feel any improvement. She took the samples and the prescription.

Knowing David would make a big issue of her taking it, she didn't want him to find out about the medication. Since Maritza took a number of daily vitamins, she combined her new pill with her vitamin schedule. There was no reason for David to know she needed an antidepressant to get through the day.

He didn't believe in taking pills. With his profession in mind, he refused any medication that wasn't prescribed by his flight surgeon and approved by the FAA. He saw too many older pilots lose their medical certificates over drugs they were prescribed. Not him. He was meticulous about working out and keeping fit. Getting in and out of the cockpit would never be a problem for him if he had anything to do with it. He watched those old jet jockeys twist and complain, throwing their backs out getting in and out of the cockpit seats. They griped about carrying those heavy flight bags and got out of breath easily. He vowed never to become one of them. Besides, a trim waist almost always ensured a great sex life.

Bettina was curious if Maritza had told her everything about her doctor visits. After taking her to Hammond when she got sick at the bookstore, she was quietly hoping Maritza was pregnant. She was almost certain of it a few days later when Maritza refused wine with dinner. Dr. Cox had told her not to drink while on the medication, and for a while she complied. After a month or so, Bettina knew her daughter wasn't expecting, but she still couldn't get a direct answer from her about the diagnosis. Maritza would just tell her she was fine, a little tired, and she was taking vitamins for that.

After the medication began to take effect, she felt better. Her panic attacks hadn't returned. As the months passed, she forgot about the havoc the attacks played with her mind and body. It wasn't unusual for her to neglect to take her medication for days, even weeks at a time.

CHAPTER SEVENTEEN

Nadia had taken most of the morning phone calls at Madame Trist's apartment, but needed to be in the gallery for a client at four o'clock. Gisela stayed at the apartment, working at her desk when her cell phone rang.

"Gisela? Hey, girl!"

"Oh, Maritza, I'm so glad you called. I'm finalizing my plans to come to the States."

"Great! Will you stay with us?"

"No, I'm bringing my assistant, so we'll stay at the loft."

"Are you sure? I mean, you haven't stayed there since..."

"I know. But I have work to do there before it's sold, and this will be the perfect time. I'll have Nadia with me, so I won't be alone."

They talked for a half hour, making plans to spend time together, until another call came in for Gisela on her other phone line.

"Take care. I'll call you once we're in New York and settled."

Gisela took the next call, hoping it was Nadia. She needed to speak with her.

"Bonjour, La Gallerie de Werner Trist, this is..."

"Madame Trist? This is Hula Schiller."

Gisela sighed, not really having time for this woman. "Yes, Mrs. Schiller."

"I just wanted to let you know that I considered the watercolor for our bank, but I've decided to stay with what we already have. My husband is just a stickler about change. I'm sure you understand."

"Certainly, Mrs. Schiller. In fact, I felt you made that clear when we met."

"Oh, no, not at all. I would like to take another look. I may be interested in a painting for our home. Could you meet with me next week, let's see, perhaps Monday afternoon? Or why don't we meet for lunch first, then take a look at the collection again?"

"I'm afraid that won't be possible, Mrs. Schiller. I'm traveling to Paris next week."

Hula thought about Nadia. *Surely, she wouldn't leave a child to run the gallery.*

"No, this week is not convenient. And I would prefer to meet with you."

"I'm sorry, but I'm afraid you'll have to wait until our return."

"And just when will that be?"

"I cannot tell you exactly when we'll open again, Mrs. Schiller. I'm traveling home first, and then we're both going to New York. This trip was just confirmed today, so the details haven't been completed."

"Well, that's a shame, Madame Trist. I suppose I'll just have to wait."

"Thank you again for calling, Mrs. Schiller. Goodbye."

Hula hung up the phone and smiled. *So, little Nadia is going to America. Why hasn't Nicolas told us that Nadia is going away? Maybe she hasn't had time to tell him. Maybe even her parents don't know.*

Perfect timing! She went upstairs and put on her new silk blouse, navy suit, and her best pearls. It was a great afternoon to pay Isabella a visit.

Nadia worked late and almost missed the evening train. On the ride home, her head was spinning. *America!* She was so deep in thought about the possibility of traveling that she forgot to check to see if the boy got off at the right stop.

As she hurried home to tell her parents, she thought about what they would say. Papa had always been so protective of her, and now she was going to venture out into the world! And Mama...she would be the difficult one.

When Nadia arrived home, she ran up the steps and into the door to find, of all things, Hula sitting in the living room with Mama.

"Nadia, come join us. Hula has stopped by for a visit to discuss the wedding."

"Hello, dear." Hula smiled at her in that plastic way Nadia detested. "Please, come over and talk with us. Let us know your ideas."

Nadia cringed at the thought of sitting down with Hula, much less talking about a wedding when there was something even more important to discuss. "Actually, you'll have to forgive me, Mrs. Schiller. I'm very tired this evening and I'd like to just—"

"Nonsense! You're too young to be tired. Come, come." She patted the cushion next to her. "Sit with us."

Mama gave Nadia a look that all daughters knew from their mothers. She sat down next to Mrs. Schiller.

"Now, Nadia, I was thinking of a large affair. You know, with Mr. Schiller's standing in the community, the guest list will be quite extensive."

"Actually, Mrs. Schiller, Nicolas and I haven't even discussed the wedding. It's all so new. We haven't had time. But I've always dreamed of a wedding at our church, just up the street. It's a lovely chapel, but it is quite small. Perhaps a more intimate wedding with a reception here at home...that's just what I'd want." Mama smiled at the thought of little Nadia marrying at the same altar where she had knelt as a young child.

"What? That just won't do, Nadia. We have a responsibility to our friends and family...it must be a larger social event. You understand, don't you, Isabella?"

"Well, I..."

Nadia stood up. "Mama, is Papa home?"

"No, not yet."

"Mrs. Schiller, it was so nice of you to drop by and show your concern about the wedding, but I haven't had a chance to speak with my parents at all about my plans. So, perhaps this discussion is a little too premature."

"Well, dear, after all, you are going to be gone for weeks. We have to get started sometime."

Gone? How did she know I was planning to travel?

"Nadia, what does Mrs. Schiller mean, that you are going to be gone?"

Hula smiled that stupid little evil grin again. "Isabella, dear, did Nadia not tell you? She's joining her boss on a trip to New York next week."

"Nadia! What's this all about?"

"Mama, hold on." She turned her attention to Hula. "And just how did you learn about this trip, Mrs. Schiller?"

"I called Madame Trist this afternoon and she happened to mention that she and her assistant would be out of the country. I was interested in purchasing one of the paintings she has for sale. That poor dear, losing her husband and having to sell his paintings. You *are* her assistant, aren't you?"

Hula stood up and walked to the door. "I see this isn't the right time to discuss the wedding, Isabella. I'll call you in a few days." Hula walked out the door, down the steps, and felt incredibly pleased that her mission was accomplished.

Mama sat, speechless.

"Now, Mama, *listen to me*. It's not what you think. I was coming home to tell you the news. I just found out today. Madame Trist must go to New York to take care of business, and she needs me to go with her. New York, Mama! Can you imagine? And she's paying for everything!"

"But Nadia, it's so far away. How long will you be gone?"

"Two weeks, three maybe. No longer."

"What? That's so long, Nadia. Too long. I'm afraid it's not possible."

"But Mama, why? It's my job, I have to go!"

Mama started to cry. She thought about Alexander, and how he had visited London with a college friend years ago, and then took a job there when he graduated. She wasn't ready for her daughter to find a future outside of their community. It seemed like only yesterday that her two children were coming home from school, sitting in her kitchen telling her about their day.

Nadia sat down next to her, feeling awful that Mama was so upset. This was going so badly, not at all what Nadia had envisioned on the train coming home. If only Hula hadn't broken the news to Mama, she could have explained it much better to her.

"Oh, Mama, I'm not a little girl anymore. I'm a grown woman."

"A soon to be married woman who should stay in the same community as her family and future husband!" Mama stood up, hurried into the kitchen, and wrapped an apron around her waist. "Go wash up, Nadia. Papa will be here soon and dinner isn't ready."

Nadia went upstairs and stared into the bathroom mirror. Tears began to stream down her cheeks. She'd never seen Mama so upset. *And what was with Hula, anyway? Why did she come over to talk about the wedding so soon? And why, all of a sudden, did she have an interest in a Christof Trist painting?*

Papa was tired when he got home, but he always looked forward to dinner with his family. Isabella told him dinner was running a little late, so he sat down to relax and read the paper.

Nadia heard his voice and came downstairs to talk to her father.

"Papa...I need to talk to you."

Papa looked as his daughter and saw that she was upset. "What is it, Nadia?"

"Madame Trist has asked me to join her on a business trip."

"Yes, in May. We've talked about that, Nadia."

"No, Papa. It's much sooner than May. Madame Trist is going home to Paris for a few days and, then...we're leaving for New York the next week. Mama's very upset with me, Papa. She doesn't think I should go.

"What do *you* think about all of this travel, Nadia?"

"Of course I want to go! I may never get this chance again to go to America. Something's come up and she needs to go to New York earlier than planned. And she's paying for the trip. She even offered time for me to shop for a wedding gown while I'm there."

"Ahh, the wedding. And what does Nicolas think of this?"

"I haven't told him."

"Don't you think you need to discuss this with your fiancé?"

"I haven't had a chance yet. I found out about this today."

"Nadia, I think if you want to go to New York with Madame Trist, then you should go, providing you discuss it with Nicolas and he agrees. If he's to be your husband, then you must include him in your plans."

"Oh, thank you, Papa!" Nadia hugged her father. "Will you please try to reason with Mama for me?"

"I'll talk to her."

Nadia went upstairs to wash up for dinner. Before she came back down, Nicolas called. Nadia told him about Madame Trist's offer to take her to New York, and he listened quietly as she spoke.

"Do you really want to go, Nadia?"

"Oh, Nicolas, I do."

"I think it's a wonderful opportunity for you. It'll be a long time before we can afford to travel."

Nicolas's calm, reasoning way was something Nadia most admired about him.

He continued to speak. "Of course, I'll miss you. How long will you be gone?"

"About two weeks, three at the longest."

Nicolas had no idea it was for such an extended period. He didn't know what to say.

"Nic?"

"I'm here."

"I know it's a long time, but she really needs my help. Besides, she's paying for everything and even told me I could take time to shop for a wedding dress. Imagine me, shopping for my wedding dress in New York!"

He was relieved to hear her talk of the wedding. "That sounds wonderful."

"Oh, Nicolas, I'm so excited. Please be happy for me."

"I'm happy for you. I love you, Nadia. Whatever it takes for you to be happy, I'm all for it. I'll miss you terribly, though."

They continued to talk about their work and plans for the weekend, until Mama called her down for dinner.

At the Schiller household, Hula overheard her son's conversation with Nadia and realized that little Nadia was telling him of her trip. She listened at his bedroom door until the conversation was almost over, and then left to go into her bedroom. She decided to take a hot bath and think her plan through. Her original strategy to befriend Madame Trist might not be necessary. After all, it sounded like she had hit the jackpot. *Nadia will be away for a while. That will give me plenty of time to change Nicolas's mind about marrying that little twit.*

She lowered herself into the milk bath and smiled. *It was perfect, just perfect.*

CHAPTER EIGHTEEN

When Nadia arrived at work the following morning, the doorman informed her that Madame Trist had an early visitor, Mr. Joseph Hofmann. He also told her that the gentleman had come to see Madame Trist around six o'clock last night when he was getting off duty.

"Really? Well, did she see him last night?"

"Yes. She had me send him up right away." Ordinarily, he would never divulge any of the tenants' information, but he felt comfortable with Nadia. Both she and Madame Trist had always been kind to him.

Nadia thanked him and hurried inside. *What could be so urgent? Other than that meeting with Hula, Madame Trist never booked appointments outside of her regular business hours.*

She took the elevator to Madame Trist's apartment on the fourth floor. She could hear someone talking inside, so she tapped softly on the door and entered quietly. Mr. Hofmann and Madame Trist were on a conference call, and she could tell it was an important meeting. Gisela nodded as Nadia entered and then turned her attention back to the conversation on the speakerphone. Mr. Hofmann was talking with another gentleman, whose voice Nadia didn't recognize.

Nadia sat at her desk and wondered what the meeting was about. His name seemed familiar to her. She checked her calendar and confirmed that there was no meeting scheduled with Mr. Hofmann. If there had been, she would have come in much earlier and prepared for the client's arrival.

When the meeting was over, Madame Trist seemed quite pleased. She introduced Nadia to the gentleman. He shook her hand, thanked Madame Trist for her time, and left, looking as though he was satisfied with the meeting's results.

"Good morning, Nadia, come and join me at the conference table." Madame Trist stretched, as though she had been sitting for a long time.

Nadia knew she had something important to discuss with her. They both settled down at the large table, and after pouring both of them a cup of tea, Gisela began to speak.

"You may have recognized Mr. Hofmann's name, Nadia." Madame Trist handed his business card to her.

Nadia looked at his card and nodded. "Oh, yes. I do now. He's with the law firm of Hofmann, Wolf and Adler. I pass by their office on my walk from the train station."

"Mr. Hofmann contacted me yesterday on behalf of a gentleman named Peter Neumann."

"Do you know Mr. Neumann?"

"Mr. Neumann owns many galleries throughout Europe, and a few in America. We're nothing more than acquaintances. My mother met him years ago at a showing in New York, and through her referral, my father did some legal work for him on several American properties. In fact, Mom also introduced Christof's work to Mr. Neumann, and he encouraged Christof to showcase his oils in several of his international locations. That was, of course, before we were married. Once we expanded our art business to Paris, Christof's paintings were only shown in our galleries."

Nadia took a sip of her tea, wondering what Madame Trist was about to tell her next.

Gisela paused. "Mr. Neumann is purchasing the Frankfurt gallery."

"Just what exactly would that mean?" Nadia was surprised to hear that Madame Trist was selling the gallery, after being so determined to close it herself.

"Once the transaction is completed, Mr. Neumann will own the gallery, including the art currently offered there." Gisela took another sip of her tea. "In fact, he wants to purchase both the Frankfurt and Paris galleries."

"Paris, too? I thought you planned to keep that open."

"I do...well, I did. At least I thought I did. He's made me quite a substantial offer for both locations."

"Are you considering his offer, I mean, for both?"

"Yes, I am. This morning I made the decision to let him purchase the Frankfurt business. We were reviewing the details with Mr. Hofmann and signing the papers to begin the process. I'm still uncertain about Paris, though. It's much closer to my heart."

"So this means you'll be leaving Frankfurt even sooner?"

"I'm afraid it does."

"How do you feel about this, Madame Trist? I mean, it's all so sudden, isn't it?"

"Yes, in fact, it all came together last night."

"After I left?"

"Well, yes. I know he'll do a fine job with this one in Frankfurt. His locations are much different. Besides the gallery itself, there will be a retail shop on the bottom floor and a coffee bar. I've seen it work at other locations. Those modern layouts attract many more customers."

Nadia couldn't believe how quickly things change in business matters.

"It sounds really...exciting." She understood Madame Trist's decision to sell the gallery and she was happy for her. It had been so difficult for her to go through the process of sorting and selling her husband's paintings to close the gallery. However, Nadia wasn't ready to let go of her as a boss.

"Nadia, I feel terrible about one thing. I know that you were looking forward to going to New York with me. But, with this offer on the table, there's much less work to be done. I'm still planning to go by myself, but for a shorter period. I can't disappoint my family. And, of course, there's Maritza. I want to spend time with her, too."

New York! Nadia had completely forgotten about the trip when Madame Trist told her the news. They were going to take inventory at the loft and decide which of Christof's paintings would be shipped to Frankfurt for the closing and which ones would be sent to Paris for the gallery. It would have been quite a project, but something that had to be done.

"All of those paintings will be shipped to Paris now, so I can have that handled for me by the New York staff."

"I understand."

Madame Trist reached over to touch Nadia's arm. "I do have good news. When I spoke with Mr. Neumann and told him how efficient you are and how well you know the inventory at the gallery, he asked if you would like to work for him on a permanent basis. That is, of course, if you're interested."

"A job at the gallery? That would be wonderful, Madame Trist! Do you think he would really hire me?"

"Yes, in fact, the job is yours. Also, I negotiated a good starting salary for you. He was happy to pay for your experience, Nadia. He also believes strongly in education. When you're ready to start school, he guaranteed me that your work schedule will accommodate your class and study time."

Nadia didn't know what to say. *A good job...and school too!*

"Mr. Neumann is a wonderful man and a close family friend of my parents. I think you'll be pleased working for him. Naturally, he'll bring in his own curator, but he or she will depend on you as well."

Nadia was thrilled! She tried to keep her excitement inside but it just wasn't possible. *A good starting salary...imagine!*

"One more thing. I'd like you to keep the ticket to New York. You can change the date to another time, or cash it in if you'd like. Maybe you and your husband can make a trip to America. A honeymoon trip, perhaps?"

"You don't have to do that."

"It's my pleasure, Nadia."

They continued to talk and make a list of everything that Nadia needed to finish while Madame Trist was in New York. When she returned from America, she would come back to Frankfurt for a short time, and then travel home to Paris. Nadia would be responsible for wrapping up Madame Trist's affairs in Frankfurt, closing her office, and shipping her belongings back to her Paris apartment.

The gallery would be closed during the transition.

"We still have a few more days together, Nadia. What do you say we celebrate your new job, take a break, and do some shopping?" Madame Trist had grown so fond of Nadia. She wanted to spend some personal time with her before she left for New York.

The rest of the day, they shopped and enjoyed each other's company. Although Nadia resisted, Madame Trist bought Nadia three suits, four blouses, scarves, shoes, and hosiery. She knew that Mr. Neumann required his staff to dress professionally, and Gisela wanted to give Nadia a fresh new start. She showed her how to interchange her blouses and scarves to create several entirely different looks. Finally, before they finished shopping, Madame Trist had her fitted in a beautiful black wool coat.

"I don't know what to say," said Nadia. She had never worn such beautiful clothes.

"Say nothing. Just consider this a bonus for all the hard work you've done for me." Gisela hugged Nadia and whispered in her ear, "I couldn't have made it through this without your help the past few months."

Nadia's eyes filled with tears. She was really going to miss Madame Trist.

Her arms were heavy with packages as she walked to the train station. *What a day it's been. Yesterday, I was going to New York. Today, I'm not going to New York. Yesterday, I worked for Madame Trist, helping her to close a gallery. Today, I have a new job offer at the gallery.* She could hardly wrap her thoughts around the changes. It was crazy!

As she waited for the train to arrive, her mind was racing. *Wait until Mama hears this. She'll be so relieved to hear that I won't be traveling. Well, at least not for a while. A honeymoon in New York sounds like a great idea. I can't wait to talk to Nicolas!*

CHAPTER NINETEEN

Nadia surprised Mama by slipping in next to her at church later that evening. After the service, they both stayed seated in the chapel.

"Mama, you don't have to worry anymore. I'm not going to New York."

"Oh, Nadia. No. I was wrong. Papa and I discussed it and I saw that I was just being too overprotective. You're a grown woman. I trust you to do the right thing."

Nadia reached over and took Mama's hand. "Thank you, Mama. It's okay. The trip has been canceled." They sat quietly for a few moments, and then Nadia rose to help Mama put on her coat. They walked home together, and she filled Mama in with all of her news from the day. As they passed a local shop window, Nadia noticed a pair of gloves.

"Let's stop in here, Mama."

Nadia purchased the gloves and handed them to Mama. "Oh, thank you, Nadia! I thought you were buying them for yourself. They're lovely."

Nadia smiled. It pleased her to be able to buy things for Mama that she wouldn't buy for herself. As they continued the walk home, Nadia held Mama's arm as they chatted about one thing, then another. It felt good to be close to her. They walked up their front steps and into the house. Papa had worked late that evening, but had arrived home to read Isabella's note that she would be at church.

"Isabella! Nadia! I'm in the kitchen." He was eating the dinner that Mama had left for him on the stove. Soon, they were all sitting around the kitchen table, telling stories and laughing together.

"What does Nicolas think of all this?" Papa asked.

"Oh, Nicolas! I have to call him right away!" Papa grinned and shook his head as Nadia headed upstairs to call him.

Hula answered the phone. Nadia asked to speak with Nicolas.

"Nicolas is out for the evening," Hula said.

"Do you know when he'll be in?"

"No, dear. He didn't say. You know how he loses track of time when he's out with his friends. If I'm awake when he gets home, I'll tell him you called."

Nadia hung up the phone. If Hula was trying to get her curiosity stirring, it didn't work. With all the excitement of the day, Nadia had forgotten that Nicolas and his father were having dinner with a client that evening. Even Hula didn't annoy her tonight. Nadia was wise to her antics.

When Nicolas arrived home, he called Nadia.

She told him her news; he was thrilled for her and happy for what it would mean for both of them. She could afford to start school earlier than expected. It was late, but he hurried over to see her, and they talked until midnight. He was happy just to be near her and wanted to stay later, but they both had to work in the morning.

She walked him outside and they kissed passionately. *How he loved this woman and couldn't wait to make her his bride!* As he drove away, Nadia watched from the front window. She couldn't remember feeling any happier than when she was with him.

CHAPTER TWENTY

To Nadia's surprise, she began working right away with Mr. Neumann, speaking by conference call each morning, keeping him updated and involved in the daily business. She was pleased with her new boss, and the people he was bringing in to Frankfurt were experienced professionals.

Mr. Neumann was thrilled to have Nadia on board because she was as good as Gisela had said. He asked for her opinion many times, and she felt honored to have input on such an important project.

The exterior of the gallery would stay the same, but the entire interior would be reconstructed to provide space for shops and a coffee bar. There was so much to do and look forward to, and Nadia couldn't wait to get to work each day.

Every evening, she and Nicolas would review what she learned. It gave him joy to see her so vibrant. She loved her job and he loved her hunger to learn new things. After they talked about each other's workday, they continued to discuss their wedding plans.

Mama and Papa felt proud that Nadia and Nicolas planned to keep with the traditional German wedding rituals. So many young people were breaking away from tradition to more modern, lavish affairs, or eloping without any family present.

For as long as Nadia could remember, there had been a clean, gallon-sized pickle jar in the kitchen pantry. It was there for her to drop in the coins she collected. Papa always emptied his pockets each evening and added them to her glass bank. "These coins will one day pay for your wedding shoes," Mama always told her.

Occasionally, Papa brought home paper rolls from the bank and Mama and Nadia worked to roll the change. Nadia loved to listen as Mama would talk of her own jar of coins that she once used to pay for her own wedding slippers. When Nadia was young, she would spend hours counting her coins and dreaming of the day she would marry her prince.

Nadia and Nicolas were relieved that everything seemed to be going smoothly. That is, with one exception: Hula.

Since Nicolas's last discussion with her, she was unusually cooperative. That alarmed him, because he knew how opposed she was to this marriage. He worried that she had something up her sleeve and that, somehow, she would manage to spoil things for his bride. If he had anything to do with it, she wouldn't have the opportunity to do so. Oskar promised him that he would keep watch on her activities, but Nicolas knew that the older his father became, the more interested he was in peace than in justice.

CHAPTER TWENTY-ONE

Gisela was happy to be back in Paris, in her own home and surrounded by the things that she loved. She was planning to leave for New York right away, but she had to postpone her trip to America for a short while longer. Although she spoke with both the Paris gallery staff and her boutique manager daily when she was away in Frankfurt, there were financial issues with the businesses that only she could resolve. Besides, she didn't mind it at all. She missed her Paris ventures. It gave her such pleasure to be there in person on the sales floor interacting with the customers.

Once everything was taken care of and she saw that both businesses were running efficiently, she packed for New York. She couldn't help but think of Maritza and how good it would be to spend some time with her. When Gisela had called Maritza to tell her she was postponing her trip, she seemed a little distant. It concerned her somewhat, but she convinced herself that her friend was just disappointed in the delay. But when she called later on in the month and told her she was coming the next week, Maritza seemed to act the same way.

Gisela's parents were relieved that she was finally coming to New York. They missed their daughter and worried about her well-being. They agreed not to do anything on a large social scale while she was home. Getting on an airplane and flying to New York alone was hard enough, without having to smile and be gracious to strangers when she was still grieving for her husband. They were disappointed that they would not be in town the first few days of her visit, due to a business commitment her father had in Miami. That was fine with her, because she was anxious to spend as much time with Maritza as possible.

When the day came for Gisela to arrive in New York, Maritza woke up early and spent extra time making sure her clothes and makeup were perfect. She tried on several outfits until she found one that fit. She threw the clothes that were too small onto the floor. *Maybe David is right. I am gaining weight. Damn!*

Maritza was finally ready to go to the airport, but left herself just enough time to park, walk inside the terminal, and wait for Gisela. She was still out of breath from rushing into the terminal when Gisela emerged from the customs area.

As they greeted each other with a hug, Gisela felt a distance between them that had never existed before. She couldn't pinpoint the cause, but Maritza just wasn't the same happy, carefree woman she knew. When Gisela remarked that she looked overly tired, Maritza felt annoyed by her comment, but she passed it off as not sleeping well.

Gisela planned to stay at the loft. However, on the drive into the city, Maritza convinced her to come and spend the night at their home since David was traveling. Maritza seemed more relaxed once they arrived back at her apartment, and they enjoyed the rest of the day talking and laughing.

After dinner, Gisela felt a little jet lag and decided to turn in early. Maritza said she was tired, too, but she was going to stay awake and wait for David's call. So Gisela excused herself and went into the guest room to get ready for bed.

Before falling asleep, Gisela called her parents at the hotel in Miami. She wanted to let them know she had arrived in New York and was staying with Maritza for the evening.

After speaking for a few minutes, Gisela asked Katharina a question.

"Mom, do you think that Maritza's okay?"

"Why do you ask that?" Her mother felt that Maritza was more high-strung than usual, but she wanted to hear what Gisela thought of her behavior.

"There's something different about her. She says the right things, but I don't think she's very happy."

"Do you mean with David?"

"I'm not sure. I've always known her to be a confident woman filled with fun and energy. Now she seems so…"

"So what, dear?"

"Defeated. I think that's the word I'm looking for, Mom."

Katharina didn't offer her opinion, although during her luncheon weeks earlier with Maritza, she noticed that Maritza had a difficult time concentrating on their conversation and seemed anxious to leave the restaurant.

The following morning, Maritza woke early and realized that she had fallen asleep in the living room. She was still sitting in the floral chair where she sat down to read the night before. She had waited for a call that never came.

On the table next to her was her favorite handbag. Gisela had given her this handbag two years ago. It was style No. 2, and Gisela knew the clean, classic lines would provide her with years of wear. Later, the following Christmas, Gisela sent her a petite wallet, which coordinated perfectly with the handbag. In the fold of the wallet, Gisela had placed a picture of the two couples. A kind tourist at La Place du Tertre had photographed Gisela, Christof, Maritza and David as they enjoyed a bottle of wine at an outside café.

Maritza reached for her handbag and pulled out her wallet. She wanted to look at the picture again. Maritza thought back to that almost perfect Paris day. She had convinced David to let her join him in Paris for a short two-day trip. While they were there, Gisela arranged for the four of them to spend the day together in the Montmartre quarter. Christof had explained to them that the Montmartre quarter once was the mecca of modern art, and that famous painters who were once penniless had lived there, including Picasso.

They had watched the street artists set up their easels for the day and occasionally sell a piece to an admiring tourist. After visiting the Salvador Dali museum and the Basilica, they enjoyed bottles of wine, freshly baked bread and cheese. Even David seemed to enjoy the day, until it was time to go back to the hotel.

This morning, Maritza stared at the picture and the good memories faded as she remembered how angry David had become that day. After a wonderful day of sightseeing, they had a huge argument over where she would stay for the evening. Maritza wanted to return with him to the hotel, but he insisted that she stay with Gisela and Christof. Her friends never knew about the argument, because David was always careful to make his point known when they were alone. She had told Gisela that she wanted to stay with them so they could spend as much time together as possible.

Tears fell as she placed the picture back into the wallet, and then slipped her wallet into the handbag and zipped it closed. *Why didn't he call me last night?*

Gisela found Maritza sitting quietly in the living room. She looked more closely and saw that she hadn't changed clothes from the day before, and that she was crying.

"Maritza?"

"Sorry, Gisela," she said as she wiped her tears. "I'm okay."

"Don't be sorry, tell me what's wrong?"

Maritza shrugged. "It's silly. Besides, I'm supposed to be cheering *you* up this weekend."

Gisela sat down next to her. "Talk to me."

Maritza thought to herself and decided she couldn't possibly burden her friend with her own problems. *After all, I still have my husband. Gisela lost the love of her life.* "I guess I just have the blues."

"How long has this been going on?"

Maritza laughed at the serious expression on Gisela's face. "Girlfriend, I'm okay, really! I just get lonely sometimes. He's gone so much."

"I know it must be hard on you. It seems like every time we talk he's on another trip."

Maritza immediately became annoyed. She snapped back at Gisela. *"Well, that is his profession!"*

Gisela wasn't sure what to say. She went into the kitchen and put on a pot of coffee. Maritza went into her bedroom and closed the door.

What could be wrong? Gisela noticed a distant look in her friend's eyes when they met at the airport yesterday. *Something was different. Maybe a little change of scenery was in order.*

When Maritza finally came out of her bedroom an hour later, dressed and ready for the day, Gisela was the first to speak. "Maritza, let's go to the Hamptons. David's out of town. My parents won't be back for a few days. What do you think?"

As Maritza poured herself a cup of coffee, she thought about getting away for a couple of days. For the first time, Gisela saw her smile. "Girlfriend, I think that's just what the doctor ordered."

Gisela called her mom and explained that she would be with Maritza at their summer house for a couple of days. They packed a few things and made plans to make the drive to the Hamptons. As they left the city, Maritza seemed to relax and become more like her usual self. By the time they arrived, the two of them were carefree and enjoying each other's company.

They settled in and walked out onto the porch. It was so peaceful. Although there was still a chill in the air, they decided to open the back windows, and the cool breeze made the curtains dance. Gisela looked out onto the bay and then closed her eyes, letting her memory drift back to her honeymoon with Christof.

Maritza poured them both a cup of green tea and they sat quietly on the porch for the longest time before either of them spoke. Gisela looked over at Maritza and saw tears welling in her eyes.

"Maritza?"

"I'm so sorry, Gisela. I don't know what's gotten into me lately. Please forgive me for taking such a tone with you earlier."

"Forget it, girl. How about taking a walk?"

"Perfect. I'll get our sweaters."

After a few moments on the sand, the girls fell into their friendship again, laughing and splashing the chilly water on each other's legs. They talked about dozens of topics, including family and friends, work, and, of course, Paris.

Maritza was fascinated with Gisela's adventures, and she loved to hear about the latest celebrities who had visited her boutique.

Up until then they both seemed to know exactly what the other person liked or needed, but lately Gisela was having a difficult time understanding Maritza. When they returned from their walk, Gisela recommended that they shop for fresh fish and vegetables for dinner. Once again, Maritza became quiet and moody during the shopping trip, rushing the purchase so they could hurry back to the beach house. This time, Gisela decided to let it pass without any comment.

After dinner, Maritza finally returned her mother's calls. Bettina was thrilled that Gisela was there and that she had coaxed her daughter to go to the beach. As far as she knew, it was her first time out of the city in months. She asked to speak with Gisela, and after a few moments she invited both girls to dinner the following evening. Much to Maritza's dismay, Gisela accepted the invitation.

The next day, Gisela took her early morning walk alone. Maritza slept until half past one. By the time she awoke, Gisela was packed and ready to leave. It took Maritza an hour to wake up and at least two more to pack her small bag. Something was terribly wrong, but Gisela couldn't get her to open up and reveal her problems. The ride back to the city seemed long and it was worrisome to Gisela that Maritza hardly spoke a word.

When they returned to the apartment, Maritza excused herself to take a nap. Gisela knocked on her door several times before she could wake her up. After several attempts, Maritza finally spoke and Gisela encouraged her to get dressed for dinner. Bettina was expecting them in an hour.

The doorman called to announce the women's arrival and Sam stood outside their apartment door to wait for them. By the time they stepped off of the elevator, Bettina had joined her husband. Sam and Bettina hadn't seen Gisela since Christof's death, and the thought of offering their condolences once again brought back painful memories to them. They had lost many friends and professional acquaintances in the attack on 9/11, and they had attended memorial services for months after the tragedy. They hugged their daughter's best friend and told her how sorry they were about her loss. Gisela thanked them. Although she tried to be gracious, it was still so painful for her to deal with Christof being gone, much less to try and talk about it. She quickly turned their attention away from her pain to their beautifully decorated apartment.

Bettina insisted on preparing dinner, even though Sam wanted to take the ladies to a restaurant. She thought it would be less awkward to stay in. Maritza had been so difficult lately, never wanting to go out with her mom and staying in that apartment day after day. Bettina was worried about her daughter. She rarely called and didn't have much to say on the phone when her mother made contact with her.

Maritza, looking at her watch, picked up the phone and tried to reach David, but the call immediately rolled to his voice mail. It was getting harder and harder to reach him by phone. "Since when do you screen your calls?" she asked in her message. "We're back in the city and at my parent's apartment for dinner. Bye."

Bettina recognized the tone of her voice. She had heard it often over the past few months. Her daughter was quiet during dinner and drank more wine than usual. As the dishes were being cleared, Maritza excused herself to make another call to David.

This time, she called the hotel directly.

"Bonjour, Hotel Parc."

"David Lane's room, please. You might have him registered under Trans-Global. Captain David Lane."

Silence fell before she heard any response.

"Madame, our policy refrains us from ringing the guest rooms after midnight. Perhaps you would like to leave a message for Monsieur Lane?"

"Yes, I certainly would. Tell Captain Lane that his wife called and wanted to know why he won't answer his fucking phone!" Maritza slammed the receiver down on the desk and looked at the shocked expressions on her parents' faces. "I don't want to hear it, Mother."

Meanwhile, in Paris, Edmond pulled out his cell phone and dialed a number that he had saved in his directory. A woman answered. Edmond spoke softly. "Bonjour. I apologize for calling at this hour, but I must ask, is Monsieur Lane available?"

David rolled over and looked at the clock. It was almost three a.m. He took the phone.

"Sir, this is Edmond at Hotel Parc. I am sorry for calling you at this hour, but you asked me to let you know if you received any personal calls. Your wife just rang, and she is very unhappy, sir. I told her of our evening phone policy, but she is quite upset. I thought you should know."

"Damn! Thanks, Edmond." He hung up the phone and motioned for Lisette to stay quiet. He called Maritza on his cell phone, but the answering machine picked up at home.

"What the hell, Maritza, waking me in the middle of the night!" David hung up the phone, thought for a moment, and dialed home again. "Where the fuck are you? You just called me, damn it. Pick up!" He continued to rant until the message line disconnected the call.

David dressed and called for a taxi. Once again, he dialed his home. When the answering machine picked up for the third time, he was furious. "Maritza...are you awake? Pick up the phone. You wanted to talk to me so badly, pick up! You fucking bitch, how do you expect me to fly tomorrow without any sleep?"

When Maritza and Gisela arrived back at her apartment, Maritza noticed the light flashing on the answering machine. They both changed into their robes and Maritza poured them each a brandy. Gisela didn't know what to say and they both had been quiet on the drive home. She had never seen Maritza act so hostile toward David or her own family.

She was always so controlled about her behavior; it shocked her to see her friend let go of her emotions.

As Maritza carried the brandy glasses across the room to sit down with Gisela, she stopped by the desk and leaned over to press "play." By the time she sat down, they were both listening to David's violent display.

Gisela looked at her friend, who was sitting with a blank stare on her face.

"Oh my God, Maritza, why didn't you tell me?"

CHAPTER TWENTY-TWO

Gisela showered, packed her clothes, and made a pot of green tea. She wasn't surprised that Maritza slept in. She had consumed a large amount of wine the night before.

She was reluctant to leave her, but she had work to do at the loft. David was due back soon, and Gisela felt they could use the time he was off to take care of their issues. She'd never seen Maritza so angry and hurt as she was last night, and she never imagined that David had such an abusive side. She had only witnessed his affection toward Maritza whenever the four of them were together. *Why hadn't she confided her marital problems to her?*

She waited quietly for her friend in the kitchen. Maritza finally came out of the bedroom and joined her. She didn't want any tea, but sat down at the kitchen bar to talk with Gisela.

"Sorry I overslept."

"Don't worry about it. I'm glad you're up, though. I have to leave in a few minutes."

"Oh?"

"I have a car coming at eleven to take me to the loft."

Maritza was glad to hear that she didn't have to drive her there. She had a splitting headache.

"Before I leave, I want to say something to you." Gisela put her hand over Maritza's.

"You've seen me through the worst moments of my life, losing Christof. If you ever need me, or need anything, all you have to do is call."

Maritza paused before speaking, then felt a little irritated and moved her hand away. "All couples have problems, Gisela."

"Yes, most do at times. I just want you to know you can count on me to be there for you."

"We're fine, *I'm fine.* Let's not talk about it anymore, okay?"

Gisela looked at her watch and saw it was almost eleven. She reached out to hug her friend, and Maritza pulled away, holding her hand up to maintain space between the two of them.

Gisela was startled, almost losing her balance as she tried to lean back again.

Realizing what she had done, Maritza felt she needed to say something. "I'm sorry. I'm just a little emotional lately."

Gisela kept her distance, telling Maritza that she understood, even though she had no idea what was happening in her friend's world to make her behave this way.

She gathered her luggage and called the doorman to see if the car had arrived. It was waiting for her, and as she began to leave, Maritza finally came to her and they hugged silently before she walked out of the door.

Gisela felt uncomfortable leaving her. Something wasn't right about the way Maritza was acting, but she couldn't pinpoint it exactly. As she slipped into the car, she had the strangest feeling that something was very, very wrong.

Maritza was glad to finally be alone. She opened her purse and unzipped the hidden pocket inside of the lining and pulled out a variety of pill bottles. Her hands trembled as she took out an assortment of pills, swallowed them with the rest of Gisela's tea, and headed back to bed.

Minutes later, Gisela arrived at the loft. She stood outside of the door for a moment before she turned the key. She knew she had to go in, but she dreaded going in alone. *Why didn't she ask Maritza to join her, just this once?* This would be the last time she would see the loft. It was the only thing left of Christof's life before her. *I can do this. I have to do this.* She took a deep breath, and in a few moments she found the courage to open the door.

She put down her bags and looked around the room. It was exactly as she had left it the last time she was there. When they married, most of Christof's personal items had been packed and shipped to their home in Paris. After that, the loft had become an art studio, with a minimally stocked kitchen. There were a few clothes and linens in the closet, and a bed for overnight use when they needed to come to New York. Paintings lined the walls, along with several boxes of Christof's art supplies.

She decided to lie down and relax for a few minutes. Her time with Maritza had been so trying, never knowing what to say or keep to herself. She closed her eyes for a moment, and then she rolled over on her side and pressed her face into his pillow. Before long, she felt that familiar wave that still came over her occasionally. Grief found its way to her once again, and the memories of life with him began to flood her mind. Christof, Paris, the honeymoon, their first Christmas, the plans they had to start a family when he returned from his last trip to New York. She wanted a child, his child, and now they were both gone forever. She began to sob, in their bed, in their loft, alone without him.

She fell asleep and woke up once when her phone rang, but she didn't feel she could talk to anyone, not just yet. She lay still, staring at the empty pillow next to her. *When are these feelings going to stop? Not only do I ache for him, I long for a child who will never be born. Our child. A boy who would look just like his father and have his love for life.* Well-wishers told her that there would be another man along the way, someone she would love and with whom she would raise a family. They didn't understand. She had had her prince and lost him. A man like Christof would never be in her life ever again. She mourned the life they had together and yearned to be with him again.

Later on, she knew she had to get up and start working, so she managed to wash her face and change her clothes. She tried to remain strong and focused to get the work done, but with so many reminders of Christof, it was impossible not to find herself in tears.

It was much easier in Paris to assure those who cared about her that she was okay. However, deep inside she had to force herself to make it through each day without him. Now, being back in New York and having to deal with remnants of his life's work, it was almost unbearable.

Her phone rang again, and this time she answered. It was her father.

"Daddy, it's good to hear your voice."

"Mom and I are back in town and we want to see you."

She looked at her watch and saw that it was almost eight-thirty. She hadn't even realized it was so late.

"How about dinner? We'll pick you up."

"It's late, don't you think?'"

"Nonsense. We'll pick you up in a half-hour."

Gisela knew her father wouldn't take no for an answer. She agreed to dinner and hurried to shower and change into her black turtleneck, jeans, and black boots. She brushed her hair back and put on a wide black headband and her silver jewelry. She added a spritz of *Amour Mystérieux* before heading out the door to meet them outside of her building.

It was wonderful to be with them. They took her to Little Italy and she felt like a child again. Her father loved the restaurants, and dining there had been a weekly event when she was growing up in New York. Many of her adult friends believed that Paris was her home, but it wasn't until she went to college there that she decided to make it her home. She was born and raised in New York, and loved the city.

After he parked the car, he told his usual story each time they came to Little Italy. He never locked his car on Mulberry Street between Spring and Canal Street, once again telling them that he could leave a stack of thousand dollar bills on the hood and no one would bother them.

The way her father said it, even as an adult she never quite understood if it was really true or not.

She looked up over her head at the old tenements with their protective fire escapes. She loved the smells and the culture of this lower Manhattan district. Christof had loved this area too, and from the time they met it was an annual event for them to attend September's Feast of San Gennaro. The streets were filled with nearly three million people over the two-week period, and the aroma of sausages, peppers, and onions sizzling on the grills beckoned those who were hungry. Sometimes he would bring his sketchpad and sit for hours, watching people flow in and out of the businesses and enjoying the variety of cuisine offered by the street vendors.

As they continued their stroll down Mulberry Street, she gazed into each restaurant's doors and windows. Many friends of her parents came out and greeted them with kisses on both cheeks. Some owners, who had known them for years, commented on how beautiful little Gisela had grown to be, reminding her how they used to feed her pasta and calamari when she was a little girl. As much as she had traveled, she still found Little Italy to be magical. She loved the cobblestone streets, flashing signs, and friendly sidewalk conversations between patrons and restaurant owners.

She started to tense up a little as they neared the restaurant she and her husband had enjoyed together. She could smell their favorite meal cooking, which was pizza, baked in a coal brick oven. After that, they would each order a cannoli, which they labeled "a cannoli to die for." She remembered how Christof loved the fact that Gisela had an appetite for good food. So many of the other women he met ate watercress salad and drank mineral water. Watching Gisela laugh, enjoying beer or wine as she reached for a second slice of pizza, made him love her even more. She was real, unlike those tall, ultra-thin models he met through his profession.

When they reached her father's restaurant of choice, up the steps they went. Her parents were greeted by their names and seated immediately. There were clean white cloths on the tables, and the owner and his wait staff rushed to surround them right away. Soon they found themselves talking, laughing, and singing with the other patrons while they enjoyed fine wine and fabulous food. The aroma of garlic, onions, peppers, and fresh basil brought back her appetite. Somehow her parents knew this was just what she needed. She felt like their child again, so safe and loved by her family. For the rest of the evening she forgot all about her sorrows and thoroughly enjoyed herself.

As they walked back to the car, Bernhard and Katharina begged her to come and stay with them, but she declined their offer. Just being with her family was enough to reenergize her for the work ahead. When they finally arrived at her building, her father walked around the car and opened the door for her. She leaned down at the car window and kissed her mother goodbye.

When she turned to hug her father, she saw the concerned look on his face.

"Gisela, are you going to be okay? I hate to leave you here alone."

"Daddy, I'm fine. I had a wonderful time with you and Mom tonight. Besides, I'll see you tomorrow, won't I?"

"You will. I should be here by noon."

"Well, then. Noon it is."

She hugged her father and waved to her mother and they drove away, so happy that the evening was enjoyable, but still very concerned about their daughter's emotional health.

Once she settled back into the loft, she realized that it was nearly one a.m. She had planned to reach Maritza before the day was over, but now it was too late to call, so she finished unpacking and prepared to go to bed. Between the jet lag, the wine, and the wonderful evening with her parents, she had no trouble falling asleep right away.

The following morning she awoke refreshed and eager to take her morning walk. On the way back, she stopped at Christof's favorite coffee shop. Everything was just the same. The staff spoke loudly and hurried to service the morning commuters. She waited to order a bialy and hot tea until she could sit at one of the little tables by the window. She remembered how Christof loved to watch the people as they rushed by the front window of the coffee shop. He always saw things differently, by angles, shading, expressions, and light, as a painter would. "Inspiration can come from anywhere, anyone, or anything and best, of course, when it is least expected," he would say to her.

She decided it was time to return to the loft and start her work. She looked through the paintings, one by one, taking inventory and admiring his work all over again. She remembered the inspirations behind his paintings. It came from many sources, such as a place where they traveled to, or a face in a crowd. He loved the innocence of children and painted them often. And there were many watercolors inspired by his love for the ocean. He loved the sea and they took many vacations to tropical places. The watercolors happened to be her favorite and were definitely going back with her to Paris.

Noon came, and her father arrived right on time. Joining him was a real estate agent, who took a look around the loft and announced confidently that she would have an offer for Gisela by the end of the day. In fact, she had a client whom she was certain would make an offer sight unseen. Property in this area was nearly impossible to find, and she assured Gisela that she could get top dollar for the loft.

Gisela looked at her father and turned to continue her task. He knew his daughter and he understood her signal. He finished taking the agent on a tour of the loft, answered her questions, and then thanked her for coming as he escorted her to the door.

After the agent left, Gisela looked up from her packing. "Thank you, Daddy."

"Honey, I know it's hard, but it has to be done."

Gisela looked around the loft and knew that it would never be the same again, not without her husband there to share it with her. It was time to sell and move on with her life.

"Will you handle the contract for me?"

"Of course I will. I already told her to contact me with any offers."

Her father insisted that she take a much-needed break, and she agreed to join him for lunch. They talked until they reached a suitable asking price for the loft. She knew she could depend on him to handle the transaction for her, and he was happy to oblige. After lunch, as he was preparing to leave, he asked her a question.

"How is Maritza doing?"

Gisela wasn't expecting that question, because he really hadn't ever spent much time around her friend.

"She's fine. Why do you ask?"

"No reason in particular, but I did notice that look between you and your mom last night at dinner when she asked how your weekend was with her."

Gisela didn't want to worry her parents about something she really didn't understand herself.

"Oh, Daddy, it's just girl stuff."

"In other words, none of my business, right?"

Gisela laughed as she walked her father to the door and kissed him goodbye.

By late afternoon she was pleased with her progress, and called to arrange for a crew to come the following day and crate the artwork. Once those paintings were shipped, everything else that remained would be donated to a local art school. After that, there were a few household items to donate to charity and then her work would be done.

That evening, her father called to let her know that the real estate agent contacted him and presented an offer for her to consider. Both she and her father felt it was quite generous; she accepted and signed the contract the following day. The buyer planned to remodel extensively, which bothered her a little. After all, this had been her and Christof's first home together. So many firsts had happened there.

Her parents kept close watch on her for the remainder of the time she was in New York. One evening, after having dinner at home with them, her father asked Gisela to come into the study and talk with him.

"Are you happy in Paris, Gisela?"

"I love Paris, you know that."

"Your mother and I would like you to come back to New York."

Gisela looked at her father and smiled. "Daddy, I have a better idea. Why don't you and Mom move to Paris?"

Bernhard laughed. "We've had this talk before, haven't we?"

"Many times, and the answer is still the same."

About that time, Katharina joined them.

"No luck, my dear. She still wants to live in Paris."

"But, darling, I worry about you so. Won't you at least *consider* coming home?" Katharina gave Gisela a look that only mothers can give. She'd seen it before many times.

Gisela sighed, smiled at her mother, and changed the subject. "Have you heard from Maritza?"

"No, I haven't." Her mother glanced at her husband before turning her attention back to Gisela.

"Is something wrong?"

"I don't think so. It's just that I've called her every day since I went to the loft, and I don't get an answer. I was hoping she had tried to reach me here."

"I saw her a few weeks ago, and she seemed a little preoccupied," Katharina said, choosing her words carefully. "In fact, I was going to mention it to you and it slipped my mind. We were talking about getting together the next time you came to visit, and all of a sudden she jumped up and said she had to leave, right in the middle of our conversation."

"She's not herself, Mom, and I don't know why." With that, Gisela excused herself and went to the phone to try once again to reach her. This time David answered.

"Hello?"

"David, hi, it's Gisela. How are you?"

"Fine, Gisela. And you?"

"I'm well, thank you. Is Maritza in?"

"Yes, but she's sleeping." Gisela looked at her watch. It was eight-thirty.

"Will you tell her I called? I'd like to see her once more before I go home."

"You're going to Paris?"

"Yes, but not for a few days. I have business to finish in Frankfurt before I go home."

David was relieved she wouldn't be on his flight. "I'll tell her you called."

Gisela thanked him and hung up the phone. She wondered if he would give her the message.

She could hear her parents talking in the other room, but when she went back to join them, their conversation suddenly stopped.

Her last day at the loft had arrived and she had just a few details to finish. The paintings had been picked up for shipping, and the last boxes were removed. Her work was done and it was time to leave. She picked up the one last small box that she had found on the closet shelf earlier in the week. Inside was a picture that had been taken at an art showing shortly after they met. Christof was so handsome and she was radiantly happy. A photographer snapped the photo and placed it in the *Times* the following day with the caption "Christof Werner Trist Seen With International Model." Christof found this hysterically funny. From that point on, he had introduced her to his friends as his girlfriend, the international model.

She folded the clipping and put it her wallet, leaving the box behind.

Gisela stood at the door and took one last look at the loft. She felt both relieved and sad. It was over. One single tear fell as she turned off the light and locked the door.

Her father was waiting for her in his car. He had planned to join her inside, but Gisela wanted a few minutes alone with her thoughts before leaving the loft for the last time. When she sat down in the car, her father winked at her. She smiled at him. He was a wonderful man, and she felt blessed to have such a loving, caring father. She reached over and handed him the key to the loft. *It's over and I'm okay.* He took the key from her and they drove to meet her mother at their apartment.

She stayed with them for the next few days before taking a flight to Frankfurt. It was comforting to be with them, and she realized just how much she missed her parents. She and Katharina shopped and took in a matinee. How she missed the Broadway productions, and especially the nervous excitement on opening nights.

She still hadn't heard from Maritza. She tried to call her one last time from the airport before she boarded the plane, but there was no answer at home or on her cell phone.

CHAPTER TWENTY-THREE

When Maritza picked David up at the airport, they didn't speak all the way home. He was in a mood, and she knew better than to annoy him any more. After they arrived home, David took his bag into the bedroom, undressed, and went to bed.

When he awoke hours later, she had dinner prepared for them. On the table were fresh flowers and candles, and she was using their good china and crystal. She knew he was still mad at her for calling and waking him in Paris, so she thought she would make up for disturbing him.

He showered and came out of the bedroom to find this romantic setting on the terrace. That put him in an even worse mood because now he had to pretend to go along with it. He went back into the bedroom and dressed for dinner.

He actually enjoyed the meal, but the conversation bored him. She had spent time with Gisela while he was away, and that was all she could talk about. Finally, he asked her to change the subject. Maritza sat there, uncertain what to say next.

For the next two days, he found ways to stay busy without her. *He wished she would just leave him alone.* Crew scheduling called and notified him of a change in his next trip. He would not be going to London as planned. Now it would be another week at home before his next trip to Paris. He logged in on his computer to look for open time. *Perhaps there was a trip open that he could pick up, or better yet, trade his next Paris trip for one sooner.* Nothing was available.

He called crew scheduling and asked to speak with Nicole. He knew she had a crush on him by the way she spoke to him over the phone. If he could reach her, he would have her add his name to the voluntary flying list, or better yet, she might get to a planner and make the change happen.

He was right. She went out of her way to help him. That afternoon, the phone rang. Maritza answered it.

"Hello, is Captain Lane available?"

"Yes, he is. Is this Erica?"

"Maritza? Hi, how are you? I haven't spoken with you since you left Trans-Global. We show that David put his name on the voluntary fly list, and we have a trip for him."

"Oh? Okay, hold on. Nice to speak with you, Erica." Maritza called for David to pick up the phone.

He finished the call and smiled. His plan had worked. He would be back in bed with Lisette by the weekend.

David came into the kitchen to talk with Maritza. "That was crew scheduling. They have a fucking schedule change for me. I have to take the Paris trip on Friday. Can you believe that? 'Junior manning' all the way up to my seniority? I can't believe they couldn't find anyone else to take the trip. I'm sorry, I couldn't say no, especially with the overtime pay."

She helped him to get his laundry done and packed again.

What he had forgotten was that she too worked for the airlines. She knew he must have contacted crew scheduling and volunteered for extra flying or they wouldn't have called him. They would never "junior man" him and force him to take a trip because it would cost them overtime. They would have put a reserve pilot on it instead of paying a higher premium to an international pilot with his seniority.

That bastard lied again, Maritza thought.

The next day, it was Maritza who couldn't wait for him to leave. He disgusted her.

She made plans to spend the afternoon shopping with her mother, and Bettina was thrilled to hear from her daughter. Later in the day, she decided to spend time with both of her parents, so she called David and said she would be in late. She was planning to have dinner with them before she came home.

David was fine with that, and he headed out to have a drink with some friends. When she arrived home that evening at ten-thirty, he was out. His bag was packed and stood near the bedroom door. She carefully picked up the bag and laid it on the bed. For the first time ever, Maritza opened the bag and unzipped each compartment, looking through his notes and travel folders, taking out a few to examine more closely. When she was done, she zipped the bag and placed it exactly where he left it by the bedroom door.

She heard him unlocking the door, so she placed the note and receipts she held in her hands into her handbag. She hadn't had a chance to read them, but she would in the morning.

He had been drinking so she avoided him. She washed her face and went to bed, wondering what was in the note she found. From her quick glance, she saw that it was handwritten, but not in his handwriting, and she couldn't wait until the next day to read it.

David crawled into bed and rolled over toward her. She wasn't about to satisfy his drunken desire tonight, so she moved away. He was angry that she moved, but didn't say much to her. Soon he was sound asleep. She rolled over slowly, got up out of bed, and picked up her handbag. She walked toward the door, watching for some reaction from him until she was out of the bedroom, then turned on the lamp in the living room and sat down to take a closer look at the crinkled papers.

CHAPTER TWENTY-FOUR

When she pulled up to the departure level and stopped the car, David slid out on the passenger side. He motioned for her to open the trunk, so she pressed the release button. He put on his jacket and hat, and then adjusted his sunglasses. She watched in the rearview mirror as he gathered his bags and placed them on the curb.

After closing the trunk, he walked over to the passenger side and leaned down to say goodbye through the open window, but Maritza wouldn't look over at him. She couldn't bear to look at him.

He shook his head, turned, and walked into the terminal. *Fucking bitch.*

She sat there in the car for a moment, thinking about how happy he was to pick up this so-called *extra trip*. She jumped suddenly, as curbside security tapped on her driver's window, indicating that she had to move the car, so she pulled away from the drop-off area.

Instead of leaving the airport, she followed the signs to the daily parking lot. It was a beautiful, clear day and the afternoon sun glistened off each jet's skin as it approached the runway. Maritza watched one aircraft after another as each one climbed into the sun, wondering what it would feel like to have the freedom of flight once more.

She sat in her car for nearly an hour before deciding to leave. As she merged onto the main road coming out from the airport, tears began to flow from her eyes. *He's not going to get away with this.* She drove until she reached the bridge that would take her high up over the river, where she could have a better view of the planes in the sky.

When she approached the curve at the height of the bridge, Maritza took a deep breath, floored the accelerator, and turned into the safety rail. All other traffic screeched to a stop, watching with disbelief as the car slammed into the rail and flipped over, plummeting into the river below.

Minutes later, Trans-Global Flight 500 was holding short of the departure runway. "Trans-Global 500 JFK tower, cleared for takeoff runway 31-left." David called for the line-up checklist. As he positioned the aircraft on the center of the runway, his hand slowly moved the thrust levers forward. "Set take-off thrust." The aircraft accelerated down the runway. "V1-rotate." David slowly pulled the control yoke back. "V2." The plane lumbered skyward. "Positive rate...gear up..."

"Trans Global 500 turn right heading 050 degrees, join the departure...contact departure control...have a good flight to Paris."

As the aircraft banked to the right to intercept the departure, First Officer Mathieu Dietrich glanced down and saw the traffic at a complete stop on the bridge. "Good thing we got to the airport before the traffic locked up on the bridge. Looks like someone decided to take a swim."

CHAPTER TWENTY-FIVE

Mathieu printed a copy of the weather in Paris and saw there was a message for Captain Lane. "You have a message here. It says to see the station manager immediately when we land."

"Damn," said David. "Another drug test? For something that the company does randomly, I sure do get more than my share of them. I just had one last month."

"Here's the current weather." Mathieu briefed David on the conditions and was told to make the announcement to the passengers. First in English, then in fluent French, Mathieu spoke over the microphone. "Ladies and gentlemen, good morning. We are making our descent into Charles de Gaulle International Airport. They're landing us to the east today, current weather...overcast skies, light rain, temperature of five degrees Celsius, forty-one degrees Fahrenheit. We're about fifty-four miles out, which, barring any unforeseen delays, puts us at our gate in about twenty minutes. On behalf of our cabin crew and Captain David Lane and myself, First Officer Mathieu Dietrich, we thank you for flying Trans-Global, au revoir."

After a smooth landing and the taxi to the gate, the chime rang for the lead flight attendant. "Yes, sir?"

"I have an appointment with the cup before I can check out. Wait by the duty-free shops; I'll be about twenty minutes." She grinned as she thought of how annoyed David would be about the delay.

"No problem, Captain." Lisette hung up the phone and looked out the cabin windows at the rain. It didn't matter that it was cold and raining. She had the next three days with David all to herself.

After the passengers disembarked, David collected his gear and headed up the jet way. Standing at the door to the gate entrance was Parker, another Trans-Global captain that he knew from recurrent flight training. "Hey, Parker, what are you doing here?" Parker met David as he entered the terminal and put his arm on David's shoulder.

"Came to see you. Let's go over here to talk." As they walked away from the gate, David said, "I just have a minute…got to make my way to the station manager's office. What have you been up to, Parker? I haven't seen you since the Miami ground school."

Just then, the station manager walked out of his office toward the two pilots. He introduced himself. "David, I'm Greg Langer, the one you're supposed to see."

"Hello, Greg, this is—"

"Yes, Parker and I just met a while ago. I hear you two go way back as friends." As they walked away from the gates down the concourse, David began to feel uncomfortable. *Maybe it wasn't a routine drug test. Did he violate air space, bust a procedure? Why was Parker here talking to the station manager?*

"Come on into my office, gentlemen." Greg motioned for them to sit down.

"What is this, Parker?"

"C'mon buddy, let's have a seat."

"What's going on?" David looked at Greg and said firmly, "If there's some kind of problem here, I'm not talking to anyone without my union rep." Greg sat quietly as Parker began to speak.

"It's not work, David. I have some bad news for you." Parker's voice began to quiver. "Maritza's been in an automobile accident. It's serious."

"How serious? What happened?"

"We don't know the details, but she was a few miles from the airport when her car went off the road. That's all we've been told."

David dropped his head in disbelief. "I need to go home; I need to get to her."

"That's already been arranged. You'll go back with me today."

David looked at his watch. "Isn't there anything sooner?"

"Sorry, buddy. Just one, and it's not direct. You'll get home faster on Trans-Global."

Greg decided to leave the two of them alone to talk. "It's going to be a while. You're welcome to wait here in my office instead of the gate. Can I get you anything?"

David shook his head, and reached for his phone to try and call home. No answer. No answer on Maritza's cell phone. No answer on her parent's phone. *Where in the hell is everyone?*

Lisette waited over thirty minutes for David, and she kept getting his voice mail when she dialed his cell phone. Something was unusual about this, and she was curious as to what it could be. She looked around the shops for another twenty minutes and then decided to go on to her apartment alone.

CHAPTER TWENTY-SIX

David boarded the aircraft early with the crew and settled in for the long flight. They had an open seat available in first class, and he was relieved to get it. At first, the crewmembers went about their normal procedures. They had been told of the situation, but were hesitant to say anything to David.

Just prior to the passenger boarding call, one of the flight attendants, Evan, stopped by to see him. He had flown many times with Captain Lane. "Have they told you how she's doing?"

"I don't know anything. Just that there was some kind of an accident and she went off the road. When I track down the son-of-a-bitch who ran into her, he's going to pay."

"Let me know if you need anything, sir." Evan saw that David was drinking bourbon, so he went to the galley and brought him back two more bottles and some fresh ice. Since David was released from duty and no longer in uniform, he could be served alcohol just like any other revenue passenger.

When the boarding process began, David leaned his head back and closed his eyes, hoping no one came to sit in the seat next to him. Fortunately, the loads had been light today and he had the row to himself.

While taxiing to the runway, routine announcements were made, including a new security briefing: "Ladies and gentlemen, I am required to make this announcement. It is TSA policy that at no time during the flight are passengers permitted to congregate in any part of the aircraft, especially in the areas around the lavatories. We appreciate your cooperation with this TSA policy."

As they took off from de Gaulle, David noticed it was still raining. He closed the window shade, reclined his seat, and put on the headsets to keep others from talking to him. His mind raced with worry about Maritza. Parker promised that when they were airborne he would contact flight operations to get more information about her condition. Not knowing any details was driving him mad.

During the flight, Parker sent word back to David a couple of times that there were no updates on her condition. Only that she had been taken to the hospital.

Once they landed in New York, David stayed with the other crewmembers through Customs. His hands shook as he pulled out his passport. Once out of the terminal, he hailed a cab to take him to his wife. He turned on his cell phone to call her parents and find out which hospital she was in.

He had several urgent messages from the Westermanns to call them. The last one was to come to their apartment as soon as he arrived back in New York.

When the taxi pulled up to the apartment building, the doorman hurried to open the door for David. He recognized David, even though he only joined Maritza to visit her parents on holidays. "Mr. Lane, the Westermanns are expecting you."

When the elevator door opened on the sixteenth floor, David felt uncomfortable. This was the first time he had been to their apartment without his wife; it felt awkward. Sam Westermann was standing at their door and at that moment, looking at his face, David knew this was much more serious than he expected.

"She's gone, David. Our daughter is gone," Sam said as tears welled in his tired, swollen eyes once again.

David heard the words but couldn't absorb what Sam was saying. He put his roller bag and hat in the corner and looked around the room full of people. On the sofa was Maritza's mother, Bettina, sobbing with her head in her hands and leaning against someone he didn't recognize.

"What happened?"

"We don't know. They say she drove off the bridge and drowned in the river."

"My baby wouldn't kill herself!" Bettina moaned. "How could they accuse her of such? It was an accident, it had to be."

David began to feel dizzy. "When?"

"Yesterday, after she took you to work."

"I don't understand." David's eyes began to well with tears and he felt himself becoming weak.

Sam took out his handkerchief and handed it to David. "Police have witnesses who say she just drove right off the bridge. Now, David, you tell me, how does one just *drive off a bridge*? There are guardrails there, David. Why didn't those damn rails keep the car on the bridge?"

Sam broke down again, furious that the police believed his daughter might have taken her own life. "David, they think she committed suicide."

"Stop saying that!" Bettina cried.

David tried to comprehend what everyone was saying. Others in the room made their way over to offer their condolences, but he just stared in the distance as they spoke to him. He was thinking back to the first officer's comments when they took off from New York yesterday "...*the traffic on the bridge was stopped...someone decided to take a swim...*" Suddenly, it all came together and he felt overwhelmed with the realization.

*Oh my God, it was Maritza. She dropped me off at the airport in the afternoon, I told her goodbye, and...*David couldn't stand anymore; he dropped to his knees. "My wife is gone, my baby's gone..."

He sobbed in uncontrollable waves of guilt. Someone David didn't know, a family member he thought, helped him to the sofa and brought him a glass of water. Sam and Bettina wanted to console their daughter's grieving husband, but they were barely able to manage themselves.

After a few hours, David realized that he hadn't moved from the sofa. Sam and Bettina were finally alone with their son-in-law. They joined him on the sofa, one on each side of him. The rest of the evening they offered their comfort to David, and then to each other, having no idea just how horribly he had treated their beautiful daughter.

CHAPTER TWENTY-SEVEN

Gisela finished her work with Nadia early in Frankfurt, so instead of flying home she decided to take the train to Paris. It had been quite some time since she last took the train, and she had forgotten how wonderful it was to look out of the window and see the countryside and villages along the way.

When the train arrived at the station in Paris, she gathered her luggage and hailed a taxi to take her to the apartment. On the ride there, she turned on her cell phone. There were four urgent messages waiting, all from her father in New York. It alarmed her that he had called so many times. She called him back immediately.

"Daddy, I don't understand. What? No! No!" Gisela screamed into the phone. The taxi driver was so shaken by the screams that he pulled over to the side of the road and stopped the car.

Gisela began to cry. "I just don't understand how something like that could possibly happen. Are they sure? I can't believe what you're telling me. Where's David?"

The taxi driver sat quietly while she spoke with him.

"I...I will, Daddy." She choked on her tears and it became difficult for her to speak. "Give me a few minutes to collect my thoughts and I'll call you back." She sank into the seat, overwhelmed with the loss of her best friend. *How could this be happening? Why? Why?*

In a few minutes, she was finally able to compose herself. She needed to be home. Gisela apologized to the driver and asked him to continue on to her apartment. When they arrived, the driver was kind enough to take her luggage up the steps to her door. She offered him a tip, but he shook his head. As he turned to walk back to the taxi, he put both of his hands over his heart, and then waved back at her. From what he could determine from the conversation, she had lost someone terribly close to her.

Gisela opened the curtains to let light into the room. She sat down on the white leather chair, feeling empty inside. Tears poured from Gisela's eyes and she looked pale. She thought of the words her father had said:

"She was in a car crash. Her car went over the bridge and she drowned." As she tried hard to process everything that was happening, her head began to hurt. She managed to walk into the bathroom and take some aspirin, and then lay on the bed and sobbed.

Some time later, she called David at home, but got their voice mail. She was almost relieved not to have to speak with him right away, but it was even more difficult listening to Maritza's voice on the message machine: *Hi, I'm David...and I'm Maritza...we're not available...please leave a message and we'll return your call.*

Gisela sat down at her dressing table and stared into the mirror. Her mother had called her moments ago, discussing travel plans back to New York, and the thought of returning to America sent her reeling. She was still so raw with emotions from going back to Christof's loft just a few days earlier.

Gisela phoned the airline and made reservations from Paris to New York. Her next call was to Nadia. She found her home number and dialed the phone.

Mama answered and called Nadia to the phone.

"Nadia, this is Madame Trist."

"Hello! Did you forget something?"

"Oh, Nadia..."

"Is something wrong? You sound upset."

"Yes." Gisela's voice began to quiver. "Do you remember me talking about my friend, Maritza?"

"Of course." Now Nadia knew something was wrong.

"She...died." Gisela could hardly get the words out without crying again.

"Oh, I'm so sorry. What happened?"

What did happen? "She was in an auto accident. Nadia, I know it's asking a lot of you, but I need you to come to Paris."

Paris! I've never been to Paris. "What do you need me to do?"

"I need you to come and look after my commitments here while I go to the States for a few days. There are two clients of Christof's who are scheduled to meet with me. Nadia, these meetings are very important and I can't postpone them. Would you consider coming here and taking over for me?"

"Oh, Madame Trist! Do you think I'm ready for that? After all, when I used to meet with the clients here you were just a few feet away..."

"Yes. You're more than ready. If you can take the train down tomorrow, we can go over my notes before I have to leave. If you have any questions, I'm just a phone call away."

She could tell that Nadia was hesitant. "Nadia, I wouldn't ask unless it was extremely urgent. What do you say?"

"Yes, yes, of course." Nadia suddenly thought of what her new boss would say. She had no way to reach him and ask for the time off from her job. "I need to check with Mr. Neumann, though."

"That won't be a problem, Nadia. I'll call Peter. He'll understand."

"Then of course, yes, anything I can do to help you."

"Then take the nine o'clock train in the morning and I'll meet you at the station when you get in. You can stay at my apartment."

Nadia couldn't believe what she was hearing. *Paris, clients, the apartment...*

"I'll call you back in a few moments, Nadia. I have another call coming in."

CHAPTER TWENTY-EIGHT

After speaking with Madame Trist again and finalizing the travel arrangements, Nadia called Nicolas. She was relieved that he was supportive of her career. Knowing that taking a train to Paris would be a new experience for her, he offered to drive her into Frankfurt. He wanted to make sure that the ticketing and boarding process went smoothly for her. It would also give him a chance to see her before she left.

She was upstairs packing when Mama came into her room and offered to help.

"Nadia, your life is moving so fast, I can't keep up with you."

"I know, Mama. It's kind of overwhelming to me, too."

"Are you sure you're doing the right thing?"

"Like what, Mama?"

"Taking this new job, enrolling in the university, going to Paris..."

"Of course, Mama. Why wouldn't I be?" Nadia took a deep breath and tried not to be angry. She laid down the sweater she was folding, walked over, and hugged her mother. "Please, Mama. I have so much on my mind. Besides, we've discussed it. Nicolas wants me to get an education and he supports my job."

Mama kissed her daughter on her forehead and left her alone to finish packing. She didn't want to tell Nadia that the longer she waited to marry Nicolas, the more time Hula had to interfere with their plans.

When she was finished with her packing, Nadia called Nicolas to say goodnight. As she settled into bed, she thought of Madame Trist and how sad she must be feeling tonight.

Gisela poured herself a glass of wine, took a sip, and opened her closet. The thought of having to change her clothes and re-pack her luggage tonight seemed overwhelming, but it had to be done. Her eyes fell on a large painting she had placed in the back of the closet. It was the New York City skyline, and Christof had painted it years ago when he decided to move to Paris with her. He wanted to remember the city he loved. After the disaster, she couldn't bear to see the painting, so she took it from their apartment and shipped it to the Frankfurt gallery to sell. When Peter took over the business, the painting was still there, so she shipped it back to her apartment and stored it in the closet.

She knelt down and let her fingertips slide across the oil strokes, as though she was tracing each skyscraper. When they reached the towers, her fingers stopped. Tears flowed as she remembered how excited he was that morning when they last spoke, and how she had tried to get in one last goodbye.

By the time she returned to Paris again, Nadia would have sold it for her. Tonight would be the last time she would see this work her husband was so proud of.

She leaned the painting against the wall of her bedroom and continued to pack. After finishing her wine and taking a hot bath, she fell asleep.

CHAPTER TWENTY-NINE

Nicolas drove Nadia to the station, and instead of dropping her off, he insisted on helping her check in and locate the platform assigned to the Paris train. She appeared relaxed and confident, but he knew better. Nicolas anticipated that she would be nervous, having never taken the train by herself out of Germany. He was right, and she was relieved that he came into the terminal with her.

When the time arrived for her to board, he could tell that she was still a little anxious. If he didn't have his own schedule to keep, he would have joined her on the trip. As they both stood up, he reached for her and hugged her, kissing her softly on her forehead. Nicolas asked her to call him as soon as she arrived in Paris. She didn't own a mobile phone, nor did anyone in her family. But he insisted that she carry his phone on this trip and told her he would get a second one while she was away.

Soon, she was next in line and a short, uniformed man looked at her boarding pass and directed her to a first class cabin. For a brief time she was alone, and then a woman and a small child joined her. Once they all settled in, Nadia introduced herself to the woman and before long they were sharing travel stories and entertaining the little girl. Nadia finally felt relaxed and was able to enjoy the ride. It fascinated her to see the towns pass by, and she wondered about the people and their lives. She loved living in Germany, but she always wondered what it would be like to live elsewhere.

When the train slowed down and they entered the Paris station, Nadia began to feel a little anxious again. She gathered her bags and walked through the terminal. Madame Trist was waiting for her, just where she said she would be standing. No matter how many times she saw her boss, Nadia was always taken aback at her beauty and sense of style.

"Madame Trist, I'm so sorry about Maritza. I know you were the best of friends."

"Thank you, Nadia. I'm so glad you came to help me." With that said, Gisela reached out to her and held the embrace for a long time. Nadia could feel her grief and see it in her face; even with the big black-tinted sunglasses she wore to hide her red, swollen eyes. Nadia was relieved to finally get to Madame Trist and help her find her way through this terrible tragedy.

The taxi ride was exciting to Nadia, and she marveled at how the streets were filled with traffic and pedestrians. When they turned the corner, Nadia had her first glimpse of the Eiffel Tower. There was so much to see and take in for a girl who had rarely been out of her small town. Naturally, she had taken the train countless times with her family as a child to Frankfurt, and then on her own to work for Madame Trist. But this city was so different. It was alive with traffic and people, stores and monuments. With every turn of the car she became more and more captivated with Paris.

They stopped first at the apartment; Nadia was overwhelmed at how beautifully decorated the rooms were. They were much larger than she imagined, and bright, with light streaming through the front windows. She loved the reds, golden yellows, and touches of black throughout the living room. She learned from Madame Trist that every room needed a touch of black to "ground it," as she would say. It was a decorator's secret, and Nadia was grateful to learn something about home design. *Soon, she would have her own little place where she could experiment with color.*

Rich fabrics and textures, mostly damasks, silk, and toile adorned the furniture and windows. Christof's paintings decorated the walls, and she recognized a few of them from a brochure she had seen at the gallery in Frankfurt. Leaning against one wall opposite the glass windows was the largest mirror Nadia had ever seen. By day, light came through the windows and bounced off the huge mirror, filling the room with sunshine.

She told Madame Trist that she dreamed of having a home she could decorate just like this. She thought about how she could possibly try to describe it to Mama and Nicolas. The kitchen appliances were all stainless steel and the counters were made of quartz. Pots and pans hung from a large rack above her head and the floor was a beautiful Italian tile. It was such a contrast from Mama's kitchen, where the family gathered and there was always activity. The Zeller kitchen was the heart of their home. Nadia wondered if Madame Trist ever used her kitchen, because everything looked so new and untouched.

Gisela took her into the guest room where she would be sleeping. She felt like a princess. It was decorated in shades of pale pink, with tulle and ribbons and white lace. She later found that Madame Trist had decorated it in those shades because Maritza loved pink, but her husband would never allow her to decorate their home with anything but neutrals. Nadia wondered how many times Maritza had actually visited Paris and slept in this room, but under the circumstances, she didn't want to ask.

In the corner was a dressing table with numerous perfume bottles. Madame Trist had collected them for years, and some looked quite valuable. The table was antique with a marble top, and the beveled mirror took on the reflection of the lace curtains. In the closet were hats and handbags of every style and color, boxed and labeled with a photograph of what was tucked inside.

There was a lovely cradle on the floor filled with pink and white ballet slippers from Madame Trist's childhood. The cradle had been hers when she was an infant, and it had been saved for her own children, but sadly Gisela and Christof didn't have enough time together to start a family. It was trimmed with white lace and pink ribbons, and made a beautiful nest for her ballet memories. Nadia thought of how Madame Trist had donated generously to the ballet company in Frankfurt.

Madame Trist took Nadia to a chic bistro, located close to the Champs-Élysées. The outside was adorned with white twinkling lights and lush greenery. Inside, large oil paintings lined the walls leading into the main dining area. Gisela enjoyed dining there frequently and had introduced it to Christof when he first joined her in Paris. She told Nadia that the restaurant was famous for its vast wine cellar and tasting bar.

Madame Trist ordered a salad of chicken liver and goat cheese. Nadia had no idea what to select from the menu, and didn't understand most of the words. Gisela quickly stepped in and suggested that she try *gratinee au cide*, which was an onion soup with apple cider vinegar and Gruyere cheese. Nadia was relieved to have her help, and she enjoyed the soup along with the buttery croissants.

Next they walked to La Boutique. Madame Trist explained that she personally handpicked the entire inventory. Nadia saw that she had wonderful taste in women's accessories. The store was feminine and very upscale, and catered to both female and male shoppers. Nadia met the staff and it was fun for her to see the ladies she had spoken with on the phone.

They were only there for a short time, and then they continued their walk to La Gallerie de Werner Trist. Nadia was amazed at the size of the gallery and the vast number of paintings on display. There were still many of Christof's works there, but he'd been determined to give other local artists an opportunity to show their paintings, so he had provided several rooms to be filled with collections from new artists just waiting to be discovered.

Nadia met Hans, who managed the gallery, and spent time wandering through the rooms while Madame Trist took care of her business details. There was one painting in particular that Nadia felt drawn to. It was of a girl, dancing in a green field, with streamers of colorful ribbons. She looked so full of joy and carefree. She asked Madame Trist about her husband's inspiration for the painting. Later, Madame Trist motioned to Hans, and after Nadia left the room, he removed the painting and waited for her instructions.

Back at the apartment, Gisela finished packing and going over details with Nadia. She was taking a late flight that evening, and before she left she wanted to make sure Nadia was comfortable and understood what needed to be done.

Once she felt satisfied that things were in order, she called for a taxi and left for the airport.

Now, all alone, Nadia couldn't believe she was standing in Madame Trist's apartment. She made sure the doors were locked and decided to turn in early. She was meeting with the clients at eleven o'clock the next morning, and she was tired from the train ride and all of the day's events.

She set the alarm and pulled back the comforter on the bed. She had never slept on such fine sheets or under a down comforter. She closed her eyes and just as she began to relax, the phone rang, startling her.

She answered the phone and it was a gentleman, confused by her voice. It was David.

"I'm looking for Gisela."

"Yes, you have her home. She's not here. This is her assistant, Nadia."

"Who?"

Nadia could tell he had been drinking. She explained herself to him again; this time David understood.

"Oh. Sorry I bothered you."

"It's no bother, sir."

Before she could say anything else, he hung up the phone.

As Nadia tried to read and make herself sleepy again, Gisela was fastening her seatbelt. The flight had been delayed for two hours. She was glad to hear the captain make an announcement to the crew to prepare the cabin. Soon, a flight attendant stopped by to pick up Gisela's wine glass and to ask for her entrée preference. Gisela decided to pass on the meal.

The flight attendant made a note of her desire not to be disturbed, and said, "If you change your mind, Madame Trist, my name is Lisette. I'll be happy to prepare something for you."

Gisela thanked the flight attendant and then reached behind her neck to adjust the pillow. Lisette handed a blanket to her and turned off the overhead light. Gisela closed her eyes, hoping to fall asleep for a few hours.

CHAPTER THIRTY

Nadia woke early and showered. She was enjoying breakfast on the terrace when the doorman called on the phone. Just as Madame Trist had planned, a staff member from the gallery had arrived at nine a.m. sharp to prepare and transport the painting to the Werner Trist Gallery. She stayed on the terrace for a few moments longer and watched as the streets came alive with traffic and pedestrians. Having lived all of her life in a small village, every small detail in this beautiful city intrigued her.

Once the painting was crated and on the van, Nadia was to join the driver on the ride to the gallery. It wasn't a long walk and Nadia felt she could have gone on her own, but Madame Trist wanted her to arrive with the painting. She watched as Hans carefully opened the crate and positioned the painting on a large easel. Next, a staff member dusted it lightly with a fine brush. The painting was magnificent, and everyone felt certain the clients would be pleased.

Nadia began to feel anxious about the transaction and hoped everything went well. Madame Trist was counting on her, and she wanted to please her with the results. When the clients arrived they were escorted to the conference room to meet with Nadia.

They were pleased with the condition of the painting. She discussed the terms of purchase with them. The gentleman tried to negotiate a lower price, but Nadia had been instructed not to allow it to be sold for less, as there were other interested buyers. Finally, the deal was agreed upon and a wire transfer was initiated to secure the funds. Although they had been expecting to meet Madame Trist, the clients were pleased with how Nadia handled the transaction.

By one o'clock, the painting had been prepared for shipping and the clients had left the gallery, satisfied with their new acquisition. Nadia spent time exploring the gallery and saying goodbye to the staff, and then walked over to La Boutique. Monique, the manager, welcomed Nadia and encouraged her to look around as she assisted the customers.

Nadia loved the fine, clean lines of the store and how it reflected Madame Trist's taste in design. There was a feeling of elegance, and she watched as Monique held a handbag as if it were fine crystal. A gentleman came in to purchase a wallet that matched the bag he bought for his wife. By the time Monique finished the sale, he had also purchased a key ring and silk scarf. After she wrapped his purchase in sheer pink tissue and placed it in their signature silver box, she thanked him by name as she walked him to the door.

"I knew he'd be back," Monique said softly as she watched him step into his taxi. "His wife had commented on how lovely the scarf was yesterday, so I put it in the back for him."

They chatted in between customers and found they had much in common. Madame Trist had hired Monique without any retail experience and trained her to handle sales in the boutique. Impressed with her ability to please the customers, she had promoted her to manager last fall.

Monique was grateful to Madame Trist for the opportunity. Gisela had no doubt in her abilities, as she had been a faithful and loyal cashier at *La Boulangerie* she and her husband had frequented each morning. Monique had served the Trist couple coffee and bakery goods ever since they moved to the apartment nearby, and they were both very impressed with her ease in handling early morning customers. She had been happy to trade in her floured apron for fine attire and make the move to the boutique, working side by side with Madame Trist.

Monique also knew of Nadia, as Madame Trist spoke fondly of her German assistant. Monique pointed out that the watercolors on display were painted for the boutique by Christof, and the lovely linens on the front tables were a gift from Maritza one Christmas. In Madame Trist's office, there were pictures of them at parties and showings. Nadia had seen photographs of Christof before, but never with the two of them together. They were a beautiful couple. On Madame Trist's desk was a picture of the two of them on a boat, sunning. The water was the most captivating color she had ever seen. It was brilliant blue with an aqua cast on the surface. They looked so happy and the picture itself could have been from a magazine.

On the desk was another snapshot of a couple framed in silver. Although Nadia felt she already knew the answer, she asked about the couple in the photograph, and Monique sighed.

"It was the last picture she had of her best friend, Maritza." Nadia stared at the beautiful blonde woman in the picture and imagined how striking the two ladies must have been together.

"Oh, she's so beautiful! I spoke with Maritza, many times, but I never met her."

"The gentleman with her is her husband, David Lane. Have you met him?"

"No, I haven't met either of them."

"He's quite a charmer, that one is."

Nadia enjoyed her time at the boutique so much that she never realized the afternoon had slipped by. It was time for Monique to close the shop for the evening. Nadia helped her bring in the displays from the sidewalk and then she left to walk back to the apartment. When she arrived, the telephone was ringing. She hurried to answer it. It was Madame Trist, wanting to know the details of the morning meeting.

Nadia was happy to hear how pleased Madame Trist was with her work, and she was quite pleased with herself. After the call, Nadia undressed and put on a robe she found in the bathroom. She called and spoke with Mama, and then with Nicolas, before taking a hot bath. She loved the plush white-initialed towels and feminine bathroom décor. There were different bottles of scented oils on the marble counter, and she smelled each one until she decided on lavender. It made her feel relaxed and a little sleepy. After the bath, she put on her gown, and made herself a pot of tea. She sat down on a pretty floral tufted chair to read. Before long, she was asleep in the chair, dreaming of owning a lovely apartment in the city just like this one some day.

CHAPTER THIRTY-ONE

Gisela sat between her parents at the memorial service. It was heartbreaking to remember her friend's anxiety the last time she saw her. She wondered if David knew how depressed his wife had been. *Had she confronted him with her suspicions of infidelity?*

After the service, Gisela spoke with David for just a few moments. There were so many people attending the funeral that there was no opportunity to talk privately with him. She did, however, speak with the Westermanns. The police had spent a great deal of time with them over the past few days trying to uncover the reasons behind their daughter's mysterious behavior.

Gisela struggled with the knowledge of her friend's depression. *Should she tell the police how upset she had been before the accident?* The Westermanns were devastated over the police chief's decision to label the tragedy "a potential suicide under investigation." Witnesses reported that she had been sobbing uncontrollably and driving erratically before making a sharp turn toward the bridge railing.

Gisela stayed at her parent's home the entire time she was in New York and she found it comforting being with her family. Every morning she got up early and took a long walk. It was the only time she insisted on being alone. However, this morning the phone rang early before she left for her walk. It was Lieutenant Adler.

"Would it be possible to meet with you this morning, Mrs. Trist?"

"Certainly, Lieutenant. Anything I can do to help."

They arranged to meet at the coffee shop in the lobby of her parent's apartment building.

Gisela was waiting for him at a table near the window when he arrived. She watched him come in from the sidewalk and walk toward her. She remembered seeing him at the funeral, and thought it was unusual for the police to take such a personal interest in a case.

As he sat down, he thanked her for meeting with him and offered his condolences.

Gisela felt her eyes begin to well again, and she reached for her sunglasses. "Thank you. She was very special. What can I do for you, Lieutenant?"

"Would you say Maritza Lane was a stable person?"

She was caught off guard by the question. *What do they know?*

"Of course she was a stable person."

The lieutenant looked down at his notes, and then up at Gisela, trying to get her reaction through the dark sunglasses.

"Would you mind removing those glasses, Mrs. Trist?" He was tired and relieved that she was cooperative. "Now, getting back, would you say she was emotionally stable?"

"Emotionally stable? What are you getting at, sir?"

"Her parents said her actions over the past month have been unlike her normal behavior. They seem to believe she was under a great deal of stress."

Gisela sat quietly and stared into her cup of tea. Finally, she spoke. "No, she was a very happy, healthy woman."

"Are you saying that you have no doubt it was an accidental death?"

"No doubt at all."

Lieutenant Adler struggled through the interview. He still couldn't get Maritza's beautiful face out of his mind. "We have witnesses who say she was crying before she hit the rail."

Gisela looked him directly in the eyes. She could see that he cared about this case. "Sir, are we finished?"

"I don't know, Mrs. Trist. Are we?"

"I think so, Lieutenant."

He expected as much. They were best friends, for God's sake. He didn't blame Gisela for covering for her friend. He thanked her for her time and left.

Gisela put on her sunglasses again and sat silently with her thoughts. *There was no way Maritza would be labeled a suicide victim.*

Lieutenant Adler had one more stop to make before getting off his shift. He arrived at the Westermanns' around ten o'clock in the morning. He walked off the elevator on the sixteenth floor and stood outside their door, taking a deep breath. This was going to be difficult for all of them. It reminded him of 9/11, and how he had been assigned to go to homes and deliver news to anxious family members. He still couldn't sleep at night, reliving that horrible tragedy whenever he closed his eyes. No amount of counseling could erase those memories from his mind.

Mrs. Westermann answered the door. Bettina looked tired, but was very gracious, offering him a cup of coffee, but he said he couldn't stay. She couldn't bear to hear what he had to say, so once her husband arrived to meet with the lieutenant, she excused herself and went into the bedroom.

Sam took the officer into the den.

"Mr. Westermann, I've tried to get in touch with Mr. Lane a number of times, but he isn't returning my calls. I wanted to see if you could get this to him." He laid a white legal box on the chair next to the desk.

Inside the box were several items the police had recovered from the car. They had been held for evidence, but they were no longer needed. It was his job to release them to the family.

"Mr. Westermann, we found no evidence that the car had any mechanical problems."

Sam stood silently by the window and stared at a bridge in the distance.

"Sir?"

"Do you have a daughter, Lieutenant?"

"No sir, I have two sons. Eleven and eight."

Sam spoke as he continued to look out the window. "Let me tell you about raising daughters. A daughter is special. You love her and protect her, and you watch her grow up and go away. But she's always your little girl." Sam reached into his back pocket for a handkerchief. He wiped the tears from his eyes and hung his head in grief.

After a minute or so, the lieutenant broke the silence. "The formal report won't go out to the public until tomorrow, Mr. Westermann. I just wanted to let you know the findings and to get this box to a family member."

"Thank you." Sam's voice broke as he tried to speak again, but he couldn't keep his emotions hidden any longer. He held his handkerchief to his face and sobbed.

"I'll let myself out." Lieutenant Adler walked through the living room and out the door. He'd been doing these kinds of things for years, but this one got to him. *She was beautiful, even as a lifeless body coming out of the water. God, I hate this job.* But he knew one thing for sure. He'd never forget her.

As he pressed the button to the elevator, he couldn't help but believe that someone had hurt her very badly. *Bad enough that it had caused her to give up on life.*

CHAPTER THIRTY-TWO

Gisela tried several times to reach David before she left New York, but without success.

She called the apartment number and his cell, but he never answered. She thought he might need some help with Maritza's things or even someone to talk to or keep him company. She had never really cared for David, although she and Maritza were the best of friends.

Before Christof died, the four of them had wonderful times together in Paris and New York. Occasionally, Maritza would non-rev on David's Paris flights. While they were in the city, Maritza stayed with her and Christof, but David insisted on staying at the hotel with the crew. He told them he thought it looked more professional for the captain to stay where the other crewmembers stayed, but now Gisela doubted that was true. Looking back, Gisela realized that David always seemed to have another agenda.

The day before returning to Paris, she made plans to meet her parents midtown for lunch. She put on her L'san suit and spritzed perfume lightly into her hair. It had been such a tense week, and at first Gisela had decided not to dine out. But her parents insisted that they meet together socially, thinking the change would do them all good. Throughout the week, her mother had been involved in a charity event and her time with Gisela had been limited. Because this was the last day they could be together, she had reluctantly agreed to join them.

Katharina and Bernhard arrived early for lunch and decided to wait at their favorite bar. He loved the legendary mahogany bar and she felt there was no better martini served in New York City. They placed their drink order and talked quietly about their concerns for their daughter. She had lost her husband and now her best friend. *Just how strong could one woman be?*

Gisela looked at the clock. It was a challenge getting dressed today and it was later than she thought. She found herself in and out of grief. One moment she was fine, and then a wave would come over her and bring her to tears. Sometimes it was over Christof, then Maritza, then of losing them both. Joining her parents at the hotel would also be difficult because she and Maritza had loved to meet there for afternoon tea. She closed her eyes and could see the two of them, chatting away over fine teas, scones, petite sandwiches, and pastries. But her parents had been dining there for years, and her father was a great fan of their steaks. She wouldn't disappoint them.

Before leaving the apartment, she put on her large black-tinted sunglasses and added another handkerchief to her bag. She was prone to tears at a moment's notice, and her eyes had stayed swollen from crying off and on every day this week.

Gisela hailed a taxi and told the driver to take her to Park, between Forty-ninth and Fiftieth. Heads turned as she walked into the luxury hotel. She was the epitome of glamour, and the doorman was particularly thankful for the scent of perfume she left behind when she passed by him.

From the lobby, she called her mother to find out where they were waiting. She smiled, loving the fact that they were enjoying time together in their favorite bar.

During lunch, her father spoke of his investments and asked how the sale of Christof's paintings was progressing. He handled all of their legal matters in the United States, but another attorney that he highly recommended was working on the sale of the gallery in Frankfurt. Bernhard saw his daughter's reaction when he spoke of Christof and realized how raw her emotions must be. He looked forward to the day when all of the galleries were sold and she could concentrate solely on her business in Paris.

Katharina asked what she could do to help her daughter through the grief that she felt. While holding her hand, she noticed her daughter's hand tremble. Gisela began to speak of her friendship with Maritza, and her parents wept with her as she spoke of their daily morning calls and the dreams they had shared to one day live in the same city and raise their children together.

They also still grieved over losing their son-in-law. He had been wonderful to them and they had considered him as their son.

After lunch, her parents went back to work and Gisela tried once again to reach David. No answer. She decided to take a taxi to his apartment. Still, there was no answer at the door.

On her way out, she asked the doorman if he'd seen anyone come in or out of the Lane apartment recently. He had, in fact, delivered a box to Mr. Lane earlier that day. Shortly after, Mr. Lane had asked for his car to be brought around.

"I know this isn't any of my business," the doorman said, "but this guy's in bad shape. He has me bring his car up to go to the cemetery everyday."

She asked that he hail a taxi for her and thanked him for the information. As he opened the cab door for her, she handed him a fifty wrapped around her business card. "Keep an eye out for him, will you?"

He nodded and closed the door.

CHAPTER THIRTY-THREE

D avid stared at the temporary marker on Maritza's gravesite. When the funeral director called to ask him what to engrave on the permanent marker, he said he didn't know yet, but in his mind he knew what should be etched in granite. *Maritza Lane, loving wife of a lying and cheating bastard. Damn! How could I have been so stupid? I'd always been careful before. Did I want her to find out by being so careless?* With all his faults, he loved her and never wanted to hurt her this way.

He knelt down and looked at what was left of the beautiful floral arrangements. It was a shame that so much money was spent on fresh flowers because the wind was blowing them apart. David touched the marker for a moment, wiping his tears with his sleeve. Finally, he stood up and turned to walk back to his car.

Standing by a taxi in the distance was Gisela. She had taken a chance he would be there. He didn't want to see anyone, but there was no way to avoid her. When he reached the top of the hill where she was standing, Gisela didn't speak. She paid the driver and walked David to his car.

David broke their silence by remarking at the coincidence of them both going to the cemetery at the same time. They both sat in his car and cried together, grieving each other's loss.

Some time later, they returned to David's apartment. He unlocked the door and threw his keys on the bar. He sat down on the couch, leaned back, and stared at the ceiling.

She sat down across from him. Looking around the apartment, she saw it was a mess. She decided to stay until he went to sleep, answering the phone and making sense of the food that had been delivered, untouched, from neighbors and friends. On the bar was a large basket of fruit, assorted cheeses, and pastries from Trans-Global, along with a warm note of consolation and a beautiful floral arrangement.

She convinced him to shower, eat a little, and get some rest. It took a while, but he finally went to sleep. It was still early when she finished cleaning the kitchen, so she decided to water the plants and tidy the living room in case visitors stopped by. She turned on the table lamp by the window and was startled to see the handbag she had given to Maritza. When she picked it up, the leather was damp, and she realized that it had been in the water with her.

A shiver ran up her spine. Next to the handbag was the matching petite wallet she had sent to her one Christmas. On the floor was a white box labeled "return to the Lane family."

When she realized the box contained items from the car, Gisela had to sit down. It made her ill to think how cold her friend must have been underwater. When she regained her composure, she opened the handbag and unzipped the hidden pouch that was sewn into the lining. She had designed the bag herself and knew where to look for belongings that might be tucked farther inside. She found pill bottles filled with a variety of pain and anxiety medications, and other loose pills in the bottom of the pouch.

The wallet didn't appear to be damaged, and the contents had been emptied onto the table. Cash, credit cards, family pictures, the usual. They were all dry, so she placed everything back into the wallet. *No need for David to have to do this.*

On the table were bits and pieces of papers that must have also been in the wallet. As she flattened them out, she saw they were shopping receipts from purchases in Paris. *Why would Maritza keep so many receipts in her wallet? They must be old because she hadn't been in Paris for some time.* Included with the receipts was a piece of crinkled notepaper with writing on it.

As she flattened the note to begin refolding it, she noticed that it was written on a familiar Parisian hotel's stationery. Something caught her eye, so she read on. *Oh, my God! Who wrote this? It wasn't Maritza's handwriting.* She picked up the receipts and looked at them more closely. David Lane was the credit card user. *Had Maritza been gathering these to confront David?*

It was suddenly very clear to Gisela. Maritza's suspicions were true. David was having an affair. Flowers, candy, silk scarves, dinners, wine… breakfast for two. All of the ingredients that make for a very romantic Parisian rendezvous, sans the wife.

Gisela reached over and turned off the lamp, closed her eyes, and leaned back in the chair. She sat for what seemed like hours, thinking of how distraught Maritza had been over the past months. *Had she been so caught up in her own problems that she didn't recognize the changes in her best friend's personality?*

Tears began to stream down her face. Even Nadia had mentioned that Maritza didn't sound like herself on the phone the last few times she spoke with her.

And the lies, the deceit! How could David look at himself in the mirror, knowing what he did? Most importantly, now that she had this information, what was she going to do with it?

CHAPTER THIRTY-FOUR

G isela turned on the bedroom light. "David, we need to talk. Wake up."

David sat up in bed. "What the hell?"

"You bastard! I hope she was worth it, David, because your little affair killed your wife!"

"I don't know what you're talking about," David said as he stumbled out of bed and put on his robe.

"This is what I'm talking about!" she shouted as she held up the note and the receipts. "She found out about it, didn't she? She knew about your girlfriend, right? You had an argument about your affair and she couldn't take it so she drove off a bridge!"

Gisela expected David to respond just as violently, but he spoke so quietly that she had to focus on his words to understand him. "She never told me she knew." He sat down on the bed and put his head down into his hands. "I never meant to hurt her."

"Did she confront you? Did you argue on the way to the airport that morning? Tell me, David!" Gisela stood across from him and waited to hear his answer.

"No, I swear. Nothing was different. It was a normal day. I never knew she even suspected that there was someone else. I only found out today when I got this box from her dad. The police left it with him. It had her things from the car. Thank God it was sealed and her parents never looked inside."

Gisela's mind raced back to the last time she was in New York. She and Maritza had talked about David's flirtatious ways with women, and she heard him rant and rave on the answering machine, but nothing else was said.

"Who is she, anyway?"

"C'mon, Gisela, leave it alone." He stood up and walked into the living room. Gisela followed him.

"Tell me, David! Was she worth making your wife go crazy and drive off a bridge?"

"She wasn't crazy."

"No, you're right. She wasn't crazy. She was depressed."

"Okay, so she was depressed. What of it? Everyone gets depressed at times, but they don't go fucking crazy and floor their car into a railing!" David glared at Gisela, wishing she would mind her own business and leave things alone.

"Did you know she was taking medication?"

"What?"

"She was taking antidepressants, David. And something else for anxiety."

"Are you sure?"

"She's been on them for some time."

David couldn't believe it. He never saw her taking any medication. Only vitamins.

He went into the bathroom. There was nothing in the medicine cabinet but aspirin. He went into the kitchen and looked in the cabinets. Only vitamins, no prescriptions.

Gisela pulled two bottles from her pockets, both full of medication. "These were in her purse, David. And there are more besides these."

He looked at the pill bottles, saw they were in Maritza's name, and found that the last fill date was three months ago. *Had she filled the prescriptions but never taken the medication? Was she hoarding them to take at once? Was she that unhappy?* This was too much to believe. *Could she have taken her own life?* He had convinced himself that it was an accident, but maybe the police were right. *Maybe she was depressed and decided to take a drive off a bridge.*

"Oh, my God." He sank into a chair at the bar and laid his head on the cold marble surface.

Gisela called her parents so they wouldn't worry. For the rest of the night, Gisela and David fought, cried, and grieved for Maritza, each in their own way. This unlikely pair comforted each other, trying to make sense of this tragedy.

When the sun came up, Gisela felt it was time to leave. She packed up the box and placed it in the hall closet. Sometime in the wee hours of the morning, David had succumbed to exhaustion and finally fell asleep on the sofa. She picked up her handbag and gathered some pictures that David said she could take, then called the doorman to hail a taxi.

When he awoke later that afternoon, he was glad to find he was alone.

CHAPTER THIRTY-FIVE

Gisela returned to Paris the following day, and although she didn't want anything else to do with him, she continued to try to reach David several times to see if he was okay. For the next few weeks, David wouldn't answer the phone or leave the apartment.

One afternoon, he forced himself to go out for a walk. His neighbors hardly recognized him. Even the doorman only saw him when a delivery was made to his apartment.

David crossed the street and walked down Fifth. It saddened him to see Christmas lights and couples rushing down the sidewalk trying to get inside where it was warm. It was bitterly cold, and he hadn't dressed properly. He looked inside a shop window and caught his reflection in the glass. He didn't recognize himself. His usual efforts to be flawless had been replaced with a sweater and jeans. His eyes were swollen and his beard was growing full. On his way back into his building, he stopped to get the mail.

When he got off the elevator, he saw a package outside the door. He unlocked the door and kicked the package inside. He never felt as cold as he did then. He managed to make a pot of coffee, pour himself a cup, and sit down to look at the stack of mail, but just threw it on top of the other unopened letters and cards. He couldn't cope with it yet.

He knew there were sympathy cards from friends and co-workers. He couldn't bear to open them. And there were Christmas cards. How bittersweet. *No one should have to open holiday and sympathy cards at the same time.*

He picked up the phone and called his sister, Jana. She was so relieved to finally hear from him. None of his family had talked to him since they came back from Maritza's funeral weeks ago. She'd tried so many times to reach him, she'd even called Trans-Global to see if he was okay. Although they weren't allowed to give out any employee information, she did find one person who was kind enough to tell her that David had requested a personal leave while he handled his wife's estate.

"David, thank God! We've all been so worried. Mom and Dad have been calling, but both your phones say the message box is full. Are you okay?"

"Yeah, I'm okay."

"David, we want you to come to San Francisco for the holidays. You need your family now, and we're so far away. With Mike and the baby, it's just too hard for me to come east."

"I think you're right, Jana." She was shocked to hear him agree. He knew he had to get out of this apartment and the city. Everywhere he looked, he saw Maritza. Her things were there. She had decorated the entire apartment and he couldn't bear to look at it any longer.

"I'll let you know something this afternoon. I have to call my work and get an okay to non-rev since I'm out on personal leave. If I can manage it, I may be able to fly out in a day or so."

They hung up and she called her parents and told them the good news. His mother cried when she heard he was actually coming to California. David had always made excuses not to come home for a visit, and with his job keeping him away most of the time, they tried to understand. He even had a two-year-old nephew, his namesake, he'd never seen.

David called the chief pilot and he arranged for him to use his flight privileges. Next, he went on-line and listed himself on a flight for the next morning. He rarely used his non-revenue benefits and it was strange to arrange to fly standby.

He found the courage to call the Westermanns and apologize for not returning their calls. He told them he was going home to San Francisco. They were glad to hear from him and thought he was making a good decision to be with his family. They were still so caught up in their own grief, and with David away visiting his family they had one less person to worry about.

Then he called Trans-Global again, this time speaking with his favorite contact in HR. He only knew her by phone, but when he needed something his flirting with her always paid off. However, today the conversation was awkward. Their relationship over the phone had changed. No more innocent jokes between them. She arranged for him to convert his personal leave to an extended leave of absence, putting him on hold only to get the chief pilot's approval. When she came back on the line and they were just about to hang up, she remembered she had something else to tell him.

"Captain Lane, you've had several callers who wanted to get in touch with you. Of course, we never divulge our employees' telephone numbers or addresses, but under the circumstances we offered to take their names and pass the messages on to you."

David didn't want to hear from anyone at work, but he listened to what she had to say. She read the list of names to him. When she was finished, she added, "First Officer Wabash has called several times to see if we've heard from you."

He was the only one on the list that David cared anything about. After he hung up the phone, he called Cannonball, and his wife answered the phone.

"Yes, David, he's here. And by the way, we didn't get a chance to speak with you at the service. I want you to know how sorry we are."

"Thank you." David hadn't spoken to anyone at the funeral. He had left that to his family and the Westermanns. He had made a point of staying away from everyone, not paying attention to anyone but his own family. In fact, he didn't even know that Cannonball and his wife were there.

"Hey, David, how are you?" It was good to hear Cannonball's voice.

David had to clear his throat before speaking. "Not good. I need to get away from New York. I'm heading out west tomorrow to spend some time with my family."

Cannonball was glad to hear that. Up until the funeral, he had never known David had any family other than his wife's parents. He never mentioned anyone else. They had spoken with both his parents and his sister's husband after the service. David's sister was also there, but she had never left her brother's side.

"What can I do for you, buddy?"

"Will you get a message to Lisette?" Cannonball didn't want any part of this, but he listened.

"I need you to tell her it's over."

"Don't you think that's something you need to do yourself?"

"No, I've caused enough problems. I don't want this messed up."

"David, I can't just walk up to the woman and tell her that. You need to call her."

He's right. I should call her.

"Thanks anyway, Cannonball."

They spoke for a few more minutes before hanging up. David looked at his watch. It was late in Paris. He went into the bedroom to pack. He picked up his roller bag and placed it on the bed. It was heavy and he realized he had never unpacked from his last trip home.

As he removed the five starched uniform shirts from his luggage, he thought about his future.

Lisette. I don't want to talk to her, but I've got to end this relationship.

I could bid for other trips besides JFK-Paris.

Okay, so I won't fly to Paris anymore.

I'll do London and Frankfurt runs.

Will I be able to cope with seeing that damn bridge every time I take off and land in New York?

Maybe I should quit my job and move away.

There's nothing left for me here in New York.

Why not be based in California?

I could fly to Tokyo, Hong Kong and Hawaii.

There's a hub in San Francisco.

No.

No way I need to be that close to family on a permanent basis.

Los Angeles, maybe, but not San Francisco.

I need my independence.

CHAPTER THIRTY-SIX

Early the next morning before leaving for the airport, David called Lisette. He had stayed up most of the night, thinking of what he would say to her.

"Bonjour. Hello? David? Is that you?"

"Yeah, it's me. How did you know?"

"I recognized the number. I didn't know what happened to you at the airport," she said. "You never showed up to meet me after the flight. Then I heard what happened. I knew I couldn't call you, but I was hoping you would call me sometime."

"Lisette, we need to talk. I've made a big mistake. I should have never gotten with you, or anyone else for that matter."

As David was speaking, so was her new lover. He had come out from the bedroom looking for another cup of coffee. He leaned in for a kiss and whispered, "Where do you keep the sugar?"

Lisette covered the phone and answered, "In my purse, Captain." They laughed as they both thought of how many of those little sugar packets they had taken from the plane.

She returned her attention to the phone. "Listen, it's okay. It was fun, but it's over."

David had heard a man's voice in the background and became enraged at the thought of another man in her apartment. "*Fun?* Is that what you call it?" So who are you with now, Lisette? My wife killed herself because of a stupid little note you wrote, and all you can say now is *that it was fun?* Fuck you, you little whore!" David threw his cell phone across the room and it hit the mirror, breaking them both into pieces.

Lisette was surprised to hear that his wife had found out about them. She hung up the phone when the connection went dead. *He must have been very careless. Stupid American.*

CHAPTER THIRTY-SEVEN

Nadia loved working for Peter Neumann and was grateful for the opportunity he had given her. The new gallery was almost ready to open and the entire staff was in place. It was sleek and modern, with lots of glass, steel, and incredible lighting. There were black sculpted seats where visitors could pause and admire the paintings. A new administrative area was constructed and Nadia had her own office. She still couldn't believe her great fortune.

Gisela visited the gallery several times during the construction period and was amazed with the renovation. Each time she came to Frankfurt, she took Nadia to lunch before taking the train back to Paris. Nadia knew she missed Maritza's friendship, and she was happy to spend time with her.

The grand re-opening was scheduled for Thursday, and Peter invited Gisela to attend. He wanted her to see the final touches before the doors were opened to the public once again. As she walked through the gallery, she was amazed at the transition. They went into his office, and minutes later, Joseph Hofmann arrived. Nadia recognized him and unlocked the door to let him in. He was the attorney who had represented Mr. Neumann when he purchased this gallery.

"Hello, Mr. Hofmann. Are you here to see Mr. Neumann?"

"Yes, I am."

"Right this way, sir." She accompanied him back to the administrative offices and knocked on Mr. Neumann's door.

Peter opened the door, and Mr. Hofmann joined him and Madame Trist.

Nadia knew something was in the works. *What could it be?*

After their meeting, both Peter and Mr. Hofmann left the gallery. Madame Trist asked Nadia to come into the office and join her at the conference table.

She told Nadia her news. "I've decided to sell the Paris gallery to Peter."

"I'm surprised," Nadia said. "I thought you had plans to keep that one for yourself."

"I did, but after seeing what a wonderful job Peter's staff did with this one, I've decided to let it go. He's the one person I trust with Christof's vision. That's why I've spent so much time here, watching the renovation as it progressed. It was a tough decision, but I've accepted it now."

Nadia fell quiet for a moment. She felt sad for Madame Trist. She knew how much she loved watching the clients admire her late husband's paintings.

"It's okay, Nadia. Really. Besides, I have to face the fact that eventually his paintings will be gone."

"Well, then, if that's what you've decided, I'm happy for you."

"The good news is that now I can devote all of my time to my shop, and that *does* make me very happy."

"It's a beautiful store." Nadia thought of how much her boutique reflected Madame Trist's sophisticated style.

"Of course, you know that it leaves me time for something else."

"Like what?"

"Your wedding plans! Tell me what's happening. Do you have a date?"

Nadia told Madame Trist about the church where she had worshiped since she was a little girl.

"I've always dreamed of a church wedding, and my girlfriends, Anna Lese and Marcella, are going to stand with me at the altar."

"Well, have you chosen a dress?"

"No, but I have a file of pictures I cut out from magazines. I haven't found exactly what I want, though. Mama keeps asking me to make a decision, because she needs time to make the dress."

"Is that something that's important to her, your mama? Does she want to make the dress?"

Nadia didn't know what to say. Mama was a lovely seamstress, but she really planned to make the dress to save on the cost. Before she could speak, Madame Trist made her an offer.

"Nadia, what would you think if I offered to buy your dress?"

"Oh, Madame Trist, I couldn't possibly let you do that for me."

Gisela's face softened. "Nadia, you'd be doing me a favor. I desperately need something positive and joyful to focus on now. Please, I want to do this for you."

Nadia wondered what her parents would say. She thought Mama might be relieved, not having to find the fabric and spend weeks sewing the dress. She didn't think Papa would mind, but he was a proud man. Maybe she should talk to them about it.

"Would you mind if I spoke with my parents tonight?"

"Of course not. I want you to. Just remember, it's something I'd really love to do for you."

Madame Trist noticed the time. "I'm sorry, I really must go or I'll miss the train." They both laughed, as Nadia was the one who usually made that statement. They said their goodbyes, with a promise to speak again the next day.

Nadia finished her workday and with the excitement of the opening tomorrow, she almost missed the train herself.

She slipped into her seat and moments later the train moved slowly out of the station. Nadia was glad to be going home. All the final preparations for the gallery opening had been exhausting. She looked around the train car and noticed that the boy was seated not far from her. He must have boarded late as well, because he was seated in a different place than usual.

After a while, she watched as he stood up and prepared to exit at his destination. He gathered his book and an apple and walked back to prepare to get off at his stop. This time, she was sitting near the door, so she finally had the perfect opportunity to quench her desire to know something about this mysterious character.

"Hello," Nadia spoke up as he came near her.

She must have startled him, because he jumped, and then looked nervously in her direction.

"Hi. My name is Nadia. I see you on the train all of the time. I just thought I would say hello. What's your name?"

"Oliver."

"Pleased to meet you, Oliver. I hope you don't think this is too forward, but I always see you carrying books. Are you attending school in Frankfurt?"

"Kind of." Oliver looked down at the floor, seemingly shy.

"Well, I attend school there also. Actually, I just started to take classes." She could see that he was uncomfortable, so she decided to stop asking questions.

The train pulled into the stop and he grinned at her as he walked out of the door.

For the remainder of the ride home, Nadia thought about Madame Trist's offer to buy her wedding dress. She couldn't wait to talk to her parents about it.

When she arrived home, Mama was in the kitchen preparing Papa's favorite pork goulash. As Nadia opened the door, she could smell the pork, garlic, and onions cooking, and she was very hungry. It was so busy at work that she didn't have time for anything other than a cup of tea.

She put on her apron and turned to see a cooling rack of *zimtstern,* a lovely cookie with hazelnuts and the flavor of lemon and orange peel. Mama had already topped them with the meringue, so Nadia knew they'd be having them for dessert.

Mama stirred the sour cream into the hot meat juices, and Nadia put the egg noodles into the boiling water. After years of cooking together, they had a rhythm to their work in the kitchen. Her brother Alex had called an hour earlier, and Mama told Nadia all they had discussed, and how she planned to make a batch of those cookies after dinner to send to him, too.

Papa's timing was perfect, and dinner was on the table in a few minutes. After Papa and Mama told each other of their day's events, Nadia felt it was time for her news.

"I have something to ask both of you."

Mama and Papa looked at each other, and then at Nadia.

"I saw Madame Trist today. She told me she was selling her Paris gallery to Mr. Neumann."

Mama shook her head. "I feel so sorry for your Madame Trist, Nadia. Too much loss in her life. I say a prayer for her every day."

Papa continued to eat his goulash.

"There's something else."

The tone of Nadia's voice caught Papa's attention and he looked up at her.

"Madame Trist wanted to speak with me about my wedding plans. She made me an offer, and I told her I had to discuss it with you."

"What kind of offer?" Papa put down his fork and picked up his tall glass, filled with dark beer.

Nadia took a deep breath before speaking. "She would like to buy my wedding dress."

"Buy your wedding dress?" Mama was surprised at such a grand gesture.

"Yes, she'd really like to, Mama. She said that it would make her feel good to buy me the dress I always dreamed of. Except, of course, if you had your heart set on making it."

Papa cleared his throat, making a kind of growling sound. Nadia knew the signal.

"Papa and I will have to discuss this, Nadia."

"Okay, but let me tell you something else. She told me she needs something happy to focus on, like our wedding."

Nadia paused for a moment. "She's had so many horrible things happen in such a short time, Mama. I think it will do her good, and...I would like to have her involved in my wedding."

"You really are fond of her, aren't you?"

"Yes, Mama, I am. She's much more than a boss to me. She's...my friend."

Mama smiled as Papa took another serving of pork.

After dinner, Mama sat at her chair, writing a note to put in the box with Alexander's cookies. Papa read the paper, and when he finally put it down, Mama reminded him of the wedding dress.

"I say no," said Papa. "We can afford to pay for the fabric to make it."

Isabella thought about her own wedding dress, which was boxed and in her cedar chest. She had taken a peek at it when Nadia first announced her engagement, hoping to show it to Nadia. But she was disappointed, because it had become fragile and discolored in a few places. The lace on her veil had fared much better, but even tiny parts of lace had begun to yellow. When she herself was engaged, she had wanted a dress that she had seen in the dressmaker's window, but it was much too expensive for her parents to buy. So she had worn the gown her older sister had made when she married. It was beautiful too, but not like the one in the window.

Isabella thought for a moment longer, and said, "George, I want to say yes."

It shocked him that she agreed with Nadia. She told him the story of her wedding dress, and the one she admired that had been so out of reach for her poor father to afford.

He had no idea. All he remembered was how beautiful his Isabella was that day. "Are you sure, Mama?"

"Yes, very sure."

Papa tapped on the sofa for Mama to come and sit next to him. They sat there together, reminiscing about their wedding day. What they hadn't realized was that Nadia had been waiting at the top of the stairs for their decision. When it became quiet, she came down the stairs and stood behind where they were seated. She leaned down with her head between them and kissed them both on the cheeks.

"Thank you," she said to each one. "You've made me so happy!"

Papa looked confused. "What is this? Have you been listening to us?"

Mama smiled, remembering how Alexander and Nadia would hide at the top of the stairs when they were little, listening in on their conversations. How she wished those days were back. Time was passing much too quickly.

CHAPTER THIRTY-EIGHT

Nadia was excited to call Madame Trist with the news. But that would have to wait until morning. Tonight, she called Nicolas, then Anna Lese and Marcella. Before she went to sleep, she thought of what kind of dress she wanted. She had always dreamed of a white, long dress, with lots of tulle and pearls. She wondered what Madame Trist would recommend for her to wear.

She pulled out the drawer on her nightstand and picked up her diary and pen. As she wrote about her day, she thought of Nicolas. She felt so lucky to have found someone who loved her so, and she couldn't wait to be his bride. She thought of his reaction when he saw her for the first time in her dress. Soon she fell asleep, and dreamed of their life together.

The day was hectic and wonderful at the same time. It was half past two before she had a chance to go to her office and call Madame Trist.

She called her cell phone first. When she didn't reach her, she called La Boutique. Monique answered and Madame Trist came to the phone.

"They said yes!"

Gisela was thrilled. "Now then, we need to start making plans, don't we?"

They both talked about how exciting it would be to make the selection, and then made arrangements to speak again once the grand opening settled down and Nadia had more time to devote to wedding plans. Gisela was relieved, because she could use some time also settling into her new routine. She was home much more now, and had begun to feel comfortable with her new life.

For the next few days on her way home, Nadia spoke to Oliver and he smiled at her. He seemed to become more relaxed each day. Before long, she found that he was sitting closer and closer to where she always sat.

As she boarded the train one evening, she thought she would try something different. "Hello, Oliver! Why don't you come and sit by me so we can talk?" It was worth a try since he seemed much less guarded than he had been a few weeks before.

He came and sat across from her. "How are you this evening, Oliver?"

"I'm okay."

She looked beside him and saw the books he was carrying. They were familiar to her, but from years ago. Mama had always read to her when she was a child, and encouraged her children to read. Nadia had been able to read much earlier than her other little friends. She still had a library of children's books that Mama bought for her and Alex during their childhood years.

"Are those books for you?"

"Yeah."

Nadia wondered why this boy was reading books at an elementary level, even though he appeared to be around twelve or thirteen.

"Wow, Oliver, those are some of my favorite books."

Oliver smiled. "They are? I like them, too. This one's really hard, though. I don't always understand the words, but my teacher says I'm doing really good."

Nadia finally understood. He was learning how to read.

"It was hard for me too, Oliver. But you have to keep trying. If you'd like, I can help you on the ride home everyday."

"You would?"

"Sure."

"I always have homework. I have to read pages and get my mom to listen to me. Maybe you could listen to me, too."

"I would be happy to help you."

"Well, you can't really help me. I have to read the pages out loud, and then you have to sign my homework paper so my teacher knows that I read it to you."

"Sure, that's fine."

"Good, because sometimes my mom is so tired, it's hard for her to stay awake."

Hmm. She was curious what he meant by that, but she had made enough progress getting to know him. Maybe later on she could ask about his mother.

From that night on, they rode the train together and he read to her. Gradually, she found out more information about his life. Oliver's father had died when he was small, and he never really got to know him. His mother had raised him alone, and he loved her dearly. She never sent him to school. They lived far out in the country most of his life, only moving near Frankfurt this year.

His mother was ill. She knew she had to make a better life for her son because the doctors told her she was never going to get better. She made the decision to move in with her family, and her sister took Oliver to enroll him in school. Because he was so far behind, the local teachers recommended a special school in Frankfurt for him to attend.

There was no money available for him to live at the school, as most children did while they studied, so one of the teachers agreed to have him in her class if his homework would be closely monitored. So, this young boy took the train every day to the big city to study, and then boarded the train to come home each evening.

Nadia's heart sank to hear him talk of his life. How difficult it must be for him to travel each day to study and then return home to care for his dying mother each evening.

The apple, he told her, was from his lunch. He took fresh fruit home for his mother to eat each day, hoping it would help to make her stronger.

On this particular evening, they boarded the train as usual. But this time he didn't want to read. He just wanted to talk. He told her that his mother's health was worsening and he was scared. Nadia did her best to comfort him. It broke her heart to see him suffer this way.

When Nadia arrived home, she went into the kitchen to help Mama. After she put on her apron, she gave Mama a long hug.

"So what makes you do such a thing, Nadia? You haven't hugged me like that since you were a child."

Nadia looked at Mama and hugged her again. This time, Mama hugged her back for just as long. Although Mama felt puzzled, it was a moment neither one of them would ever forget.

That evening when Nicolas came over, they sat on the front steps and Nadia told him all about her little friend on the train. Tears fell from her eyes when she told him about Oliver's mother and her illness.

Nicolas listened to her story, and when she was finished, he told her that he wanted to meet her young friend. He also hoped to make a difference in the boy's life. He had been so fortunate to grow up with advantages in education.

"I promise you, Nadia. We'll figure out something to help Oliver."

Nadia leaned against Nicolas and breathed a sigh of relief. *Together, maybe they could make a difference in young Oliver's life.*

CHAPTER THIRTY-NINE

Nicolas was very attentive to his beautiful Nadia, and she loved the time they spent together. When she decided to start taking classes, he helped her to register for them and took her to lunch to celebrate her accomplishment. When he had time, he traveled with her by train to Frankfurt and took her on tours of the university. By the time of orientation, she was already familiar with the campus.

Mr. Neumann was supportive of her desire for education, and he allowed her to work her schedule around her classes. She did well in her first semester, and Nicolas was proud of her. And she loved him. *She loved him!* Nadia felt lucky to be marrying someone so loving and supportive, and she was committed to being the best wife she could be for her husband.

She was also busy making wedding plans with Mama, and with Madame Trist's help everything seemed to be going smoothly. That was, with one exception. Hula. No telling what she might come up with to spoil things. Mama worried all the time about it, but Nadia assured her that Nicolas was keeping watch over his mother.

Following traditional German wedding rituals, the wedding would span several days, beginning with the civil ceremony at the courthouse, with only their family present. The official marriage vows would be taken there because, under German law, it was not legal to marry only in a church. The *Standesbeamte* (German for *Registrar*) would perform the thirty-minute ceremony for the couple. This would be Hula's only opportunity to stop the union, but Nicolas had warned his mother that if she caused any problem for them at the courthouse, he would never speak to her again. Of course, knowing Hula, it would take more than that to stop her.

Three days later, the church ceremony would take place. This wedding would be much larger than the civil ceremony. Mama and Papa had been born in the village and knew most of the community. Nadia worried that Papa's modest income would not go far to pay for the party afterward, but Mama assured her that it would be fine. In fact, many of their family members and friends wanted to contribute to the fun. Klaus and Helga, lifelong friends of Mama and Papa, offered their restaurant for the party after the wedding. They happily accepted their offer, and it meant much to Nadia and Nicolas because they had spent many date nights at their restaurant.

Klaus had seen Nicolas on occasion in his pub, so he contacted Oskar and suggested that the boys come to his pub to drink and have fun before the wedding. This tradition for bachelors in German culture was called *Junggesellenabschied.* He felt honored to host Nicolas's last chance for male fun!

When Oskar received the call from Klaus, he began to think about the salary he paid George at the bank. Surely, this wedding would drain him of his modest savings, so he decided to talk with Hula about hosting the dinner after the civil ceremony. Hula was furious! *After all, it was the bride's father's responsibility to pay for the wedding, a wedding that she didn't even want to take place!* Hula ranted and raved and threatened Oskar with various ill doings, but he wouldn't budge. So, Hula finally agreed to call Isabella that morning. Of course, after he left for work, she never placed the call.

When Oskar mentioned the dinner to George a few days later, George had no idea about the plans made by Hula and Isabella. Isabella had never mentioned it to him. When Oskar saw his wife at dinner, he asked her about it. Hula told him that she had made the call, but no one was home. It had then slipped her mind and she forgot to call later on.

Oskar stood up at the table, went into his study, and picked up the phone. "George, I want you to let us plan the dinner for the wedding on the twenty-first. Before you say anything, I want you to know we won't take no for an answer."

George didn't know what to say. He hadn't had a chance to talk to Isabella and he was a little confused over the whole situation. "Well, thank you, Mr. Schiller. In that case, we accept."

"Now, George, we're about to be family. Don't you think it's time you called me Oskar?"

"I would like that, Oskar."

"Now, go tell your lovely wife that we'll take care of the family dinner. *Auf Wiedersehen.*"

"Auf Wiedersehen."

George went into the kitchen to talk to Isabella. She was icing a cake, and he couldn't help but steal a taste of the creamy caramel mixture. She couldn't believe that Hula would offer any help with the wedding, but, after George told her the series of events that day, she decided it would be best to accept the offer graciously. George still felt a little uneasy. After all, he felt responsible for his daughter's wedding costs. It was one thing for Madame Trist to take care of the wedding dress, but now his boss was involved. He didn't like it, but the commitments were already made.

Oskar stayed in his study for some time, leaning back in his leather chair and nursing a drink he poured after calling George. Hula was pacing in their bedroom, wondering what Oskar would say to her when he finally came upstairs for the night.

She decided to change and get ready for bed. *Still no Oskar.* So, Hula devised a plan. She put on her robe and headed downstairs. "Oskar, dear," she said outside of the door to the den. He didn't answer, so she tapped on the door and looked inside. Oskar was sitting in his chair with his back to her.

"Did you call Isabella?"

"Yes, I spoke with George. It's all settled."

"Good, then. You know, I tried to reach Isabella a number of times, but she never answered the phone."

Oskar sat silently, waiting for her to lie some more.

"Oskar, I'm so happy to do this for Nadia and Nicolas."

What else will she come up with?

"Dear, I'll call Isabella tomorrow and see if she wants to meet me for lunch."

How he wished she would just go upstairs and leave him alone.

"Well, I'm ready to turn in. How about you?"

Oskar spun around in his chair, and it startled Hula. "I know that you never called Isabella. Furthermore, I know that you never intended to host this dinner. You listen to me, Hula. If you do anything else to try and ruin this wedding, I will never forgive you. Nor will your son. And I will make sure of that."

Hula closed the door and went into the kitchen. She put on a pot of water and took a teacup from the corner cabinet, carefully, because her hand was trembling. He didn't scare her. *The old bastard.* Her hands trembled because she was angry. Too angry to speak back. *Let him think he upset me. Let him believe I'm going to give in to him.*

She drank her tea and thought of what her next move would be.

CHAPTER FORTY

N adia called Madame Trist and described what she considered to be her perfect wedding dress. Gisela had such a good time talking with her and giving her suggestions. It reminded her of the times she and Maritza would talk about the season's fashion trends.

Gisela began working on it right away, contacting L'san. When she told him of Nadia and described what she was looking for, he sketched what would eventually be Nadia's wedding dress. When L'san felt it was time to be introduced to the bride, Gisela made the arrangements for both Nadia and Nicolas to come to Paris for her bridal fittings. She was happy to pay for them to come to Paris for her appointments with the designer, and she looked forward to seeing the young couple, so much in love. Nicolas was a handsome young man, and she could see how much Nadia adored him. She watched as he looked at his bride-to-be when he spoke to her. She could see the love and devotion in his eyes; it made her think of Christof. Nicolas made Nadia feel loved and wanted, just as Christof had made her feel when they were together.

One morning, Gisela went for her walk as usual, and as soon as she arrived at La Boutique, the phone rang. It was Nadia.

"Nadia, how are you?" asked Madame Trist.

"Oh, just fine! I received the package from L'san yesterday. It's beautiful, exactly what I needed! Mama cried when she saw the suit on me."

Nadia had mentioned to Madame Trist that she couldn't find anything appropriate to wear to the civil ceremony. Gisela had understood. It would be difficult to find the right suit off the shelf. Since Gisela had asked L'san to personally create Nadia's wedding gown, she had called him right away to see what he could do for her. He made her a beautiful white silk suit with a matching hat, using the measurements that he already had on file for her gown.

"I'm so happy you like it, Nadia. How is the fit?"

"Perfect. Like a glove."

Gisela had known it would fit perfectly. She had stopped by his salon to see the suit before it was shipped to Nadia. *She's right,* she thought now. *It was beautiful.* While Gisela was there, she also looked at Nadia's gown. It was almost finished, and they were only days away from preparing to steam it before it was packaged and shipped to her. As a favor to Gisela, L'san had assigned his top designer, Paolo, to handle the details.

Nadia had one special request. She asked if the lace from Mama's wedding veil could be worked into her headpiece. Although L'san would have never considered such a thing in the past, he did it as a special favor for Gisela. She had spoken with Paolo personally, and he agreed to combine the old lace with his to make the headpiece and veil a sentimental keepsake.

"I just don't know how to thank you, Madame Trist. You have been so wonderful to me."

"Just be happy, Nadia. And live each day to the fullest."

CHAPTER FORTY-ONE

When Gisela had first come back to Paris after Maritza's funeral, she was relieved to be back home. She needed time to herself to deal with the loss of her best friend. For a few days, she had stayed at home, cleaning and reorganizing to keep her mind busy. Nearly every day, she wanted to pick up the phone and call Maritza. She just couldn't get her mind around the fact that she would no longer be on the other end of the phone. She was used to telling her everything about her day, and now, whom would she turn to with her joys and fears?

Gisela knew from losing Christof that her life would go on without her friend, just as it had when she lost him. She forced herself to go about her day in spite of her sadness. She thought of how Christof and Maritza would be upset with her if she didn't go on with her life in a positive way. In time, she knew if she focused on other things, eventually she would have a real sense of herself in this world again. After all, she had a business to run and family and friends who loved her. And she had Nadia's wedding to look forward to, which made her very happy.

So Gisela began to spend her days at the boutique, taking care of the business and meeting with vendors. She had missed her customers while she was away, and it was wonderful to be able to chat with them again. Many of her most loyal customers had heard that she lost another one close to her, and they made an effort to tell her how sorry they were for her loss. She felt so fortunate to have so many wonderful people in her life, including Monique. She was pleased with how Monique had managed the boutique over the past few months. With the weeks she spent in Frankfurt and the trips to New York, Gisela hadn't had much time to focus on the boutique. So one of the first things she did when she came back to work was to give Monique a bonus and a two-week holiday.

In the evenings, she spent time catching up with her friends or relaxing at home. Gisela loved to entertain, and when she felt like socializing again, she invited small groups over for the evening. She and Christof had loved to cook and they had their kitchen equipped with state of the art appliances. However, now that she was alone, she rarely prepared a meal just for herself. It was much more pleasurable to prepare her favorite dishes to share with friends.

About one month after her return to work, her parents came to visit her in Paris. They were pleased to see how well she was doing. She told them all about Nadia and her family, and how she was helping Nadia with her wedding dress. Katharina could hear the joy in her daughter's voice when she spoke of the young German girl. She saw that by helping Nadia with her wedding plans, it had also helped her own daughter cope with the changes in her life.

Gisela was relieved to hear news from them about David, because it was impossible to reach him by phone. Her parents had dinner with the Westermanns before they left for Paris. David had sold the apartment after a few weeks and moved to the West Coast. He had taken a personal leave, and when it was time to return to work he requested a transfer to be based in San Francisco. Gisela was pleased to hear that he lived near his family. She hoped he had changed his life for the better.

Katharina and Bernhard saw that Gisela was happy, and they were so relieved to find her at peace. She was in a good place now and they felt comfortable leaving her and returning to New York.

Early one morning, Gisela was preparing for her daily walk. After putting on her jogging shoes, she picked up her keys and headed out the door. The morning air was cool and crisp, and it made her feel energized. Before long, her fast walk turned into a run. She hadn't had this much energy in some time, and it felt great to feel this alive again.

As she neared her boutique, she slowed her pace so she could stop and take a look at the window displays. Monique had done a fabulous job decorating them last night, featuring the latest group of leather bags that had arrived the day before. She noticed that Monique had used the tablecloths that Maritza had given to her. For the first time, she was finally able to smile at reminders of her best friend rather than be tearful. She started to run again, and when she rounded the corner, Gisela glanced upward. Looking up through the metal beams of the Eiffel Tower, she saw a jet flying high over Paris.

As she continued on her run, she thought about the lives of the passengers on board that plane. *Who are they? Where are they going?* She remembered that Maritza once told her that in an emergency situation, each passenger (and crew member) is referred to as a "soul on board."

She had learned so much about working for the airlines from Maritza. If she didn't have her shop, she might have even considered a job like Maritza once had. *International travel. Meeting new people. Fantastic destinations. Flight benefits. Maybe one day, I might just decide to turn the shop over to Monique and make a change with my life.*

Gisela laughed at her wandering thoughts of becoming a flight attendant. *After all, why not just fly the thing herself?* Anyway, there was no need to make such a huge change in her life. Right now, she was happy to be where she was…here…in Paris.

CHAPTER FORTY-TWO

It was a busy evening in the Zeller kitchen. Nadia, Marcella, and Anna Lese were at the wooden farmhouse table in the kitchen making wedding decorations, and Mama was baking. The girls were laughing and enjoying themselves so much that they didn't hear the phone ring.

The call was for Isabella. Another friend of hers from church was volunteering to string flowers. She was happy to have more help. On the day before the wedding, her lady friends from church were stringing flowers to decorate the couple's car and cutting lengths of white ribbon to place in Nadia's bouquet. It was traditional for the bride to give each driver one of these ribbons to tie onto their car antennas after the wedding for the drive to the evening celebration. Isabella felt so thankful to have such a wonderful church family.

After taking the call, she joined the girls at the table. They were making little organza bags to hold the rice for the guests to throw at the bridal couple as they left the church. The tale was told that the number of grains of rice that remained in the bride's hair reflected the number of children the couple would have.

"Nadia, are you planning to have children?" asked Anna Lese.

Isabella was interested in her answer, too.

"Yes, of course." Nadia was busy cutting organza in perfect circles. "How many, I don't know. Hopefully, I won't have a dozen grains of rice in my hair!"

The girls laughed and Isabella smiled. It was so nice to have the laughter of young people in their home, and Nadia was thoroughly enjoying herself.

There was a knock on the door and Isabella walked into the living room, drying her hands on her apron. She looked out the curtain. *Hula! What does she want?*

She removed her apron and opened the door. Hula walked in with an arrogant attitude.

"Isabella, I'm here to discuss dinner plans. Is this a convenient time?"

"Yes, of course. Come in and sit."

Hula looked at the sofa with that disapproving glance she had, brushed it off with her gloved hand, and sat down. "Would you like some coffee, Hula?"

"No, thank you. Now, Isabella, how many people are we expecting?"

"Let's see." Isabella had to think for a moment. "About twelve."

Nadia and her friends sat quietly in the kitchen and listened to the conversation. Hula had no idea they were listening.

"Twelve! I thought it was just immediate family." Hula seemed annoyed and questioned Isabella even further. "I'm planning to have dinner at my house for eight. Do what you can to get it to that number; otherwise, I simply cannot be responsible for the meal."

Isabella didn't know what to say. She and Nadia had already told the family they would be invited to the evening celebration.

"Well, I really must be going, Isabella. We'll speak again soon."

With that, she turned and walked out the door.

Nadia picked up the kitchen phone and called Nicolas. Just last week, he had moved into an apartment not too far from where Nadia's family lived, wanting to make sure that Nadia would be near her family when they married. This, of course, had infuriated Hula because she hoped to have stopped this love affair before it reached the point that he moved away from home.

Nicolas picked up the phone and paced as he heard of the discussion his mother had just had with Isabella. Before they finished the call, there was a knock on the door. Nicolas opened the door to find Hula on the steps.

This is going to save me a phone call. "I'll call you back, baby."

Instead of letting her in, he put on his jacket and went outside to talk with her. He motioned for her to sit on the bottom step. She shook her head, so he sat down without her.

"What do you want, Mother?"

"That's all I get, Son? I haven't even seen your new apartment."

"I don't know what you expect from me. You disappoint me, Mother. You embarrass me. But the real problem is that you hurt Nadia. She's going to be my wife, whether you like it or not."

"Nicolas, I love you. I want the best for you. I don't think Nadia deserves a man like you."

Nicolas stood up and looked her in the eyes. "I think you should leave now."

Hula's eyes welled with tears. "How can you speak to me that way? I'm your mother!"

"I realize that. But I'm getting married. This will be our home. I don't want you coming here unless you can show respect to my wife." With that said, he turned to walk up the steps.

"Nic, wait! Why should I show *her* respect? I gave you every opportunity to meet someone who would help you out in life. If you want to run the bank, you need a wife who is polished and sophisticated. You need a woman with status in this community. Nadia's nothing. Nothing!"

"Leave, Mother!"

"Just one more thing, Nicolas. If you continue with this idea to marry that girl, I won't be at the wedding. I won't have any part of it."

With that said, Nicolas opened the door and slammed it behind him.

He called Nadia back and assured her everything would be okay. He also called his father and told him of his mother's visit to see Isabella and her latest attempt to cause trouble for them.

A few minutes later, he looked outside and saw that her car was gone. He grabbed his jacket and went down to the pub to join his friends, but he was in no mood for a good time.

CHAPTER FORTY-THREE

Hula cried all the way home. She had taught Nicolas social skills, surrounded him with fine things, made sure he had a great education, and, other than Nadia, made sure he only met women from prominent families. She never dreamed he would look twice at the little girl of a common employee! Daughter of George and Isabella Zeller? *Never!*

Pulling into the driveway, she noticed the lights were on inside. It was too early for Oskar to be home and she didn't see his car. He said he would be working late. When she went inside, Oskar was waiting for her. She walked past him and went upstairs to pull herself together.

"Woman! You take as long as you like. I'll still be down here waiting!"

Hula sat down at her vanity table and looked in the mirror at the woman staring back at her. She looked tired and her eyes were red. She brushed her hair, removed her makeup, and changed into a robe. After about twenty minutes, she came back downstairs.

Oskar was sitting in the living room waiting for her. When she finally came into the room and he could see her, he was surprised. *No makeup?* She hadn't let him see her without makeup for years. She actually looked better with a clean face and her hair down. For a moment, he remembered the woman he fell in love with so long ago.

"Oskar, what is it? I really have a terrible headache and want to turn in early."

"I spoke with Nicolas. It seems that you've been busy. Haven't you?"

She didn't respond.

"Answer me!"

"I don't know what you want from me, Oskar."

"How could you do this to your son? *Our* son? You're refusing to come to the wedding, I hear. And what about the dinner afterwards? Why are you limiting the number of guests?" Oskar stood up and came closer to Hula. "Mark my words, woman. You're about to lose your son."

Hula stared at Oskar as tears streamed down her face.

"And Isabella! She's a good, honest woman. You've treated her like she's beneath you for years."

"Yes, let's not say anything about the perfect Isabella!"

Oskar became enraged. "Woman! This time you listen to me!"

For once, Hula was actually afraid of him.

He told her of his unhappiness for years. How he hated to come home to her. How her controlling, demeaning nature had come between them years before. And how he hated himself for allowing her to dominate his son's life.

But things were going to change. Tonight.

Hula sobbed until Oskar almost felt sorry for her. He managed to walk away from her and compose himself. It felt good to finally confront his wife.

He picked up the phone and called Nicolas, but there was no answer. *He's probably at the pub with his friends.* He had hoped to stop by the pub tonight and join his son for a drink, but his time was better spent here.

He went back into the living room to find Hula sitting silently in the chair. This time, she had something to say to him.

"Oskar, I love you and I love Nicolas."

"I've never questioned that you love your son. I believe that you do. And he loves Nadia. If you love your son like you say you do and you want him in your life, you have to accept Nadia into the family. As for us, it's just you and me now, and things have to change. In some ways, I blame myself for allowing you to rule our lives for all these years."

"Hula," he continued in a tone that she'd never heard him use before, "this has to stop. I'm not a young man anymore, and I can't live this way. No, let me rephrase that. I won't live this way."

Hula began to sob again. Oskar knew he should try to comfort her, but he couldn't find it inside of him to do so. He sat with her for a few minutes, and then went into the kitchen to find something to eat.

She was exhausted. It had been too much tonight. *One thing's for sure, though. Oskar is right about Nicolas.* She'd never seen him so angry. *I'd better start cooperating with the wedding plans or I'll lose my son forever.*

CHAPTER FORTY-FOUR

Hula thought hard for days about what would happen to her relationship with her son if she didn't attend the civil ceremony. She decided that it was worth the gamble. She told Nicolas that she would not attend, nor would she have any part of the dinner afterwards. To her surprise, both Oskar and Nicolas seemed relieved.

"Do what you want," they both told her. "The wedding is taking place whether you're there or not."

When the day came, the Zeller house was filled with happiness and excitement. Alexander came home for the week to join in the festivities. He and some friends took Nicolas out to the pub to enjoy his last night of bachelorhood. Before the evening was over, Oskar and George joined them. They had a great time, and Nicolas was thrilled to be surrounded by friends, his dad, and a new brother and father-in-law.

The next morning, Nadia struggled to get her hair up and pinned in a twist, but in the end it was Mama, along with almost a can of hairspray, styling it into a perfect French twist. After she put on her suit and placed the silk hat on her head, she looked at herself in the mirror. She seemed so grown up all at once. Mama walked past her room and stopped to admire her beautiful daughter. Then Papa joined her at the door. Last of all, Alexander peeked at his sister. The entire family cried as they embraced the bride-to-be.

Nadia and her family arrived at the courthouse, and Nicolas and his father were waiting for them. When Nicolas opened the car door and Nadia stepped out, he was so taken back that he almost lost his footing on the curb. She was so beautiful to him, and his heart swelled with pride at making this gorgeous woman his bride.

The civil ceremony was scheduled at the courthouse at three o'clock, and it started right on time. As was customary, the only people attending a courthouse wedding were the couple, their parents, and the siblings.

The ceremony lasted longer than the thirty minutes they estimated, and Hula never showed. As far as Nicolas was concerned, it didn't matter. He was marrying the woman of his dreams.

As they walked down the steps of the courthouse, Nicolas kissed his bride publicly for the first time. Nadia was now Mrs. Nicolas Schiller, and that made them both very, very happy.

Oskar was so proud of his son. He had grown into a fine man, and this marriage would make him settled and centered. There was no talk of Hula, although secretly everyone probably felt relieved that she made no effort to stop the union. Dropping out on her commitment for dinner plans didn't affect the celebration either. Mama's close friends stepped in and had dinner waiting at home for everyone. It pleased Nadia even more to have the celebration at home, not at a fancy restaurant or in Hula's dining room.

Hula stayed at home, pacing and looking at the clock. It was over now. That little twit got what she wanted. Hula decided to go on to the party. Hopefully, Oskar would cover for her and go along with the headache excuse she used to keep her from the service.

She put on her favorite suit and shoes, and drove to the Zellers' home. Everyone had arrived from the courthouse, and the house was filled with laughter and music. Hula walked up the steps. Before she could knock, Oskar stepped out to stop her from coming inside.

"What are you doing here?" he said as he took her by the arm and tried to escort her back down the steps.

"Oskar, you're hurting me!" She pulled away and stood still. "I feel better now. I want to join the party."

"If you say or do one thing to upset anyone inside, you'll have to deal with me."

Mama opened the door. "Hula, how nice of you to join us. Come in."

"Well, thank you, Isabella. I'm sorry I wasn't at the courthouse. I had a nasty migraine. I'm feeling much better now." She turned toward Oskar with a look that dared him to speak otherwise.

"Well, good. Join us."

Hula walked through the door; the first one to see her was Nicolas. "Mother, what brings you here?"

"Congratulations, darling," she said as she hugged him. She looked around the room and found Nadia who, incidentally, she thought looked lovely in the beautiful silk suit. "Nadia, come here and let me congratulate you!" Nadia looked at Nicolas and he shrugged his shoulders, as he too questioned her motive. Hula hugged her just as she had Nicolas.

"Forgive me for not being here sooner. I suffer from migraines, you know. But nothing was going to keep me away from this celebration today."

Okay. So she came to the party. Oskar thought she deserved an award for her acting today. As long as she behaved, he wouldn't say anything. He was grateful for George and Isabella's graciousness, allowing her to come in their home like nothing had ever happened.

The evening was wonderful and everyone enjoyed being together as a family. That was, everyone but Hula. No one would be the wiser, as she was on her best behavior. She had to do this for her son if she wanted any kind of relationship with him in the future.

Although Nadia and Nicolas were officially husband and wife, they had agreed to wait until the wedding ceremony that weekend to stay together at their new apartment.

Oskar and Nicolas were the last ones to leave. They stopped by the pub for a drink before Nicolas took his father home.

"So, Dad, what do you think?"

"About what, Son?"

"Mother. I didn't expect her to show up tonight. Do you think she's changed her mind about us?"

George thought about Hula and her unpredictable nature. *One thing about her, she did love Nicolas. Maybe she was genuine. Maybe not. But there was no reason to have Nicolas think the worst of his mother.*

"Son, I know your mother wouldn't have come unless she wanted to be there."

Nicolas finished his drink and suggested that they call it a night.

When Oskar arrived home, Hula was already in bed. He went into his study and poured himself another drink. One down, one to go, he thought. Surely, she wouldn't cause trouble at the church. What good would it do? The kids were already married.

CHAPTER FORTY-FIVE

Nadia felt privileged to own such an elegant gown. It arrived the day after the civil service, and she could hardly contain her excitement as she opened the box. Since she traveled to Paris for the fittings, Mama hadn't seen anything but the sketches and fabric swatches. Nadia waited until Papa and Alexander were out of the house to bring the dress into Mama's bedroom. She removed the tissue and gently laid the gown across her mother's bed. When she was satisfied that it was properly displayed, she called down for her mother to come upstairs to see her dress.

Mama washed her hands and put on her glasses. She had never seen such a creation. The silk was finer than any fabric she had ever touched. There were pearls and crystals hand sewn to the corseted bodice, and the full tulle skirt ballooned high on the bed. Nadia untied the ribbon on another box and showed Mama her headpiece. Mama looked at it carefully and her eyes welled with tears. "My lace, Nadia. I see my lace woven in with the new lace." It was a surprise to Mama, and she was overwhelmed with the thought that her daughter would be wearing lace from her original wedding veil.

"Oh, Nadia, I can't believe it!" Mama hugged her daughter tightly.

"Mama, don't cry."

Isabella tried to speak, but her voice broke as she said, "Happy tears, Nadia, only happy tears."

Isabella held on to her daughter thinking of her little girl again. She couldn't believe she was married. *It seemed like yesterday that I was in the park, watching Alexander and Nadia play with their friends.* When she finally felt she could let her go, she kissed her on the forehead and suggested that they sit down for a while, reviewing the church wedding details one last time.

They carefully re-hung the wedding dress and placed the veil back into the box. Nadia carried her treasures to her room and joined Mama downstairs in the kitchen. There they sat for hours, talking and laughing mostly, and finally reviewing the plans until they both were satisfied that every detail had been addressed.

Nadia kissed Mama goodbye and headed upstairs to change clothes. She and her friends were meeting for dinner. She called Nicolas to say goodnight early, since she didn't know how late she would be out with her friends. She was happy to hear that her brother was with him. They were such good friends, and it warmed her heart to know that he and Nicolas were now family.

"Nadia, I have an idea."

"What's that?"

"How about us having a candlelight dinner tomorrow evening in our new home?"

"I think that's a wonderful idea, Nicolas."

"Alright, then. Let me plan the meal."

Nadia agreed. Nicolas was a wonderful cook. *At least Hula taught him how to take care of himself.*

They continued to talk and Nadia lost track of time. She finally had to get off the phone, or she would be late. Anna Lese and Marcella would be looking for her soon.

"I love you, Nicolas."

"I love you too, Mrs. Schiller."

In the background, she heard Alex yell out, "Hang up, Mrs. Schiller, we're trying to watch a movie!"

Nadia laughed at her brother's antics. She still couldn't get used to hearing her new name.

CHAPTER FORTY-SIX

Nicolas left work early and spent the afternoon preparing dinner. When Nadia arrived, the apartment was warm and inviting. There was a fire dancing in the fireplace, and candlelight on the table.

"Oh, what are we having?" It smelled wonderful, and she was thrilled to have a husband who knew his way around the kitchen.

"*Wienerschnitzel*, and if you're a good girl, for dessert you can have a slice of home-made German chocolate cake."

"*You made a cake?*"

Nicolas laughed. "Don't get excited. Marielle made it for us."

Marielle was their next-door neighbor and a good friend of Isabella. When she heard that they were officially married, she baked a cake for them to enjoy. As soon as she saw Nicolas come home today, she had delivered it with a note of good wishes for the couple.

The pork was cooked perfectly, and Nadia thoroughly enjoyed the meal. When they were finished, it was difficult for her to watch him clear the table without her help, but he insisted that she relax in the living room.

Moments later he brought dessert and coffee on a tray that Mama had given to them. They finished their meal, enjoying the warmth of the fire and some quiet time together.

This time, she insisted on taking the tray into the kitchen, and she returned to sit next to him on their new sofa. They sat quietly, both thinking of how wonderful this felt. Just one more day, and they would come home to each other every night for the rest of their lives.

Nicolas broke the silence. "Nadia, you know I've loved you since I was a boy. You've made me the happiest man in the world, becoming my wife. I want you to know that I will always be there for you, love you, and take care of you." With that, he reached under the sofa cushion and retrieved a black velvet box. "I have something for you."

She loved surprises! Inside, she found a pearl necklace with matching earrings. "I hope you'll honor me and wear them tomorrow."

Nadia couldn't be happier with his gift. She had thought about asking Mama if she could borrow a pair of her earrings tomorrow, and now she had her very own pearls to wear with her wedding gown.

"Of course! Oh, Nicolas, they're just beautiful. I won't try them on tonight, but, yes, I'll be wearing them when we meet at the altar." She leaned toward him and they kissed for the longest time. He pulled her closer to him and they both sank into each other's arms. As they sat there together in front of the fire, dreaming of the next day's events, both of them knew they were exactly where they were supposed to be. Together. Forever.

Nicolas was deep in thought. He knew that he would do whatever it took to protect his wife. No one could ever come between what they had. Not even his mother. He would make sure of it.

Over the crackling fire above the mantel was the painting Nadia had admired in the Paris gallery. Madame Trist had it delivered to them as a housewarming gift. It was the painting of the girl dancing in the fields, with streamers of colorful ribbons. Nadia later learned that Christof had titled the painting *Joy*.

It was late, and Nicolas drove Nadia home. Her parents' home was a quick walk away, but there was no way he would let her walk home so late in the evening. When they reached the top of the steps to her door, he held her close and whispered in her ear, "Mrs. Nicolas Schiller, will you be my bride tomorrow, once again?"

They laughed at the thought of getting married for the second time in a week. But Nadia had always dreamed of a church wedding; her husband was happy to accommodate her.

She thought that everyone was asleep, so she went upstairs quietly and closed her bedroom door. Not long after that, she heard a knock. It was Papa.

"Come in, Papa."

They sat down on the bed together and Papa told her he had realized that evening would be her last night at home. His little girl was married, off now to live a life on her own with her new husband. She thought she caught a tear in his eye, and it made her begin to well up with her own tears. "Oh, Papa. You know, you'll always be the first man I loved. And I still do."

They cried and then laughed and hugged each other for a long time.

"Okay, off to bed, young lady. You need your beauty sleep. Tomorrow's a big day!"

"Goodnight, Papa."

"Goodnight, my Nadia." As Papa closed the door, he felt a tinge of sadness, for this was the last night she would be in his house, and the years seemed to have gone much too quickly. On the way to bed, he passed Alexander's bedroom. It was good to have him home for the wedding. He was proud of Alexander and the life he had made for himself. *Now, if we could just find a wife for him!*

He walked into his bedroom and saw Isabella, sleeping soundly. As he removed his robe and slipped into bed beside her, he felt blessed to have such a wonderful wife and family. *Life had been good to him.*

CHAPTER FORTY-SEVEN

In the morning, Nadia woke early to the aroma of sausages cooking in the kitchen. She hurried downstairs and found Mama at the stove, busy preparing breakfast. Nadia was hoping to spend some time alone with her before Papa and Alexander came downstairs. She hugged Mama and reached for a clean apron.

"No, not today, Nadia. It's your wedding day! No work for you in the kitchen. You have years of that ahead of you."

"Oh, Mama, I'm not like you. Nicolas can make his own breakfast."

"Nadia!"

"*He can* and *he will*. We both have jobs, and I'll be leaving for work before he has to be at the bank." Nadia thought for a moment and laughed. "Actually, he'll be home before I will. He can start dinner, too."

Mama shook her head, thinking how different this generation was compared to her own.

"Come on, Mama. Let's sit down and have a cup of coffee together before the men come downstairs."

Isabella turned down the heat on the sausages, poured them both a cup of coffee, and joined her daughter at the kitchen table.

They sat quietly for a moment, enjoying the rich, creamy coffee. Mama decided to break the silence. "So, how are you today, *Mrs. Schiller?*"

"Oh, Mama!" Nadia laughed. "Stop calling me that. Every time I hear it, I think of Hula."

Hula. Mama worried that Hula might try to cause trouble today, but surely she wouldn't be foolish enough to make a scene at church. *She had too many friends who would keep watch on Hula to prevent that from happening.*

"Mama? What are you thinking about?"

"My beautiful daughter. I'm so proud of you, Nadia. I'll miss having you here every evening. We've spent a lot of time in this old kitchen, haven't we?"

"We have, Mama. And I'll never forget our time together." Nadia reached over and placed her hand over her mother's hand. "I love you so much."

When Nadia saw tears in her mother's eyes, she left her chair and knelt down next to her. She laid her head on Mama's lap, and soon she felt her mother's touch. Mama was stroking her hair and twirling her curls in her fingers. How she wished she could turn back time to when her son and daughter were little children. Back then, her own mother used to tell her those were her best years, and now she realized just how true her late mother's words were.

When they heard footsteps upstairs, they dried their tears with Mama's apron and hurried to finish the breakfast meal. Mama had peeled apples earlier that morning, and now she dropped them into the hot buttered iron skillet, adding sugar and allspice just before they were tender. In the meantime, she heated the pan for the eggs and put the *brötchen* into the oven. Nadia set the table and called the men to come down for breakfast.

Papa looked at both of his children, once again sitting at the family table, laughing and carrying on as they had years ago. He felt so proud to be their father. When he caught a glance from Mama, he winked at her and she smiled back. It was a good day in the Zeller home, and one George and Isabella wouldn't ever forget.

When they were finished, Mama gave the men jobs to take care of and was surprised at how well they cooperated. She and Nadia went upstairs to finish their preparation for the wedding. They took one last inventory of all the accessories Nadia would need to take with her to the church. Nadia wanted to dress at the church so there would be no chance that Nicolas would see her before the wedding. When the ladies were satisfied that they had everything packed and ready to go, Mama went into her bedroom to shower and change.

Nadia looked around her room one last time. Mama was turning it into a sewing room. It had taken some time to convince her to make the change, but she had finally realized that she could use the space to sew and that the light from the window would be perfect for quilt work. Papa even agreed to put shelves in for her and build a custom cutting table.

But right now, it was filled with boxes and baskets of her clothes and items she had collected over her almost twenty years. She noticed there was a new box that Papa had found in the basement. She lifted the lid, and inside it were dolls and their tiny clothes that Mama had made for them with scraps from other sewing projects.

Since she was a little girl, Papa always bought her a doll for Christmas and on her birthday. As she grew older, he continued to buy her dolls, but they were collectible dolls. Her birthday was coming up in a few days and, now that she was married, she wondered if he would still buy her those porcelain dolls. She felt thankful that her parents had given her such a wonderful childhood.

She put the lid back on the box and decided it was time to get ready to go to the church. She couldn't believe the day had finally arrived. Today, she would have the church wedding she always dreamed about and give her heart once again to Nicolas.

Just then, the doorbell rang and it was Anna Lese and Marcella. Nadia couldn't believe how beautiful her young friends looked in their gowns. Madame Trist had helped Nadia to choose dresses for her attendants that complemented her wedding dress. The dresses had a low back with a lace-up bustier bodice. Mama stopped by Nadia's room to see the girls in their dresses, but they all turned their attention to the lovely Isabella. Nadia had never seen her mother so elegant and glowing. Her dress was an ice blue full-length sheath, with a sophisticated beaded jacket.

"Oh, Mama, you look so beautiful!" Isabella turned around to show the beading that delicately accented the silk fabric behind her shoulders.

As the girls complimented her, she joked, "Wait until you see the bride. I'm just her mother."

While the ladies continued to admire each other's gowns, Nadia finished drying her hair. Soon they were ready to leave for the church.

Alexander drove Nadia and Mama to the church, and the girls followed. Nadia called Nicolas to make certain he was at home before she stepped out of the car. Once everything had been carried into the church, Alexander went home to finish dressing and return with Papa in about an hour.

Nadia stood in the children's worship room and carefully slipped into the dress for the first time since the final fitting. It fit her perfectly. Mama, Anna Lese, and Marcella stepped back to admire the bride. No matter how many times she had shown them the sketches, none of them were prepared for what they saw. The silk bodice and full tulle skirt made her look like a princess. In the back, it was corseted and tied to accent her tiny waist. Pearls and crystals were hand sewn onto the bodice, and the sweetheart neckline framed her face perfectly.

She opened the velvet box that Nicolas had given her last night. She put on the pearl earrings and fastened the pearl necklace around her neck. When Nadia looked at herself in the mirror, she couldn't believe her reflection. *I feel like a princess! I can't wait for Madame Trier to see this lovely gown on me! And Nicolas...will he think I look beautiful?*

CHAPTER FORTY-EIGHT

Gisela took the train from Paris to Frankfurt, and by the time she rented a car and drove to the hotel, it was almost midnight. She knew it was too late to call Nadia and let her know she had arrived, so she set the alarm for seven o'clock. That would give her plenty of time to enjoy an early morning walk through the streets of Steinheim and enjoy some sightseeing before the wedding.

Before going to bed, she unzipped the L'san garment bag and hung up the dress she planned to wear at the wedding. She'd never worn this particular one, but thought it would be perfect for the event. Gisela remembered from their shopping trip that lavender was Nadia's favorite color, so she asked L'san if he would take this cream dress and add lavender beading around the jewel-neck collar. Not only did the designer add the beading at the neckline, he also trimmed the edge of the cap sleeves and the jacket collar with the same gorgeous beadwork. She couldn't have been happier with the results.

Gisela went to bed dreaming of her little friend and the life she hoped Nicolas would provide for her. She slept well, and woke up refreshed before the alarm sounded. She waited until seven-thirty to call Nadia to let her know she was there, and to find out what time she should meet her at the church. She had promised Nadia that she would help her put on her gown and make sure everything was just right before she walked up the aisle. Nadia seemed relieved to hear that she was there, and it made Gisela feel warm inside to be needed again.

Nadia suggested different streets for her morning walk, and she followed her directions. Gisela loved the historical buildings and on some corners, she felt as though she had stepped back in time. She came upon a park, where children were laughing and playing. Parents were gathered together talking and enjoying the good weather. There was such a feeling of community here, and she understood why Nadia and Nicolas wanted to make this their home.

Later on, back at the hotel, she stepped out of the shower and saw her reflection in the mirror. She was smiling, and for the first time in weeks she felt wonderful. She hadn't realized until then just how important this wedding was to her.

She applied her makeup and dried her hair. She hadn't had it cut in months and it was quite long, cascading down her back. Fortunately it was still silky and shimmering. She slipped on her dress and the fit was perfect. She had lost a few pounds and naturally L'san had his assistant make a few alterations to the dress before she picked it up. The jacket also fit perfectly and, for the first time, she noticed the lavender beading he had also added to the sleeves.

She put on her heels, picked up her satin bag and took one more look in the mirror before leaving her room. She smiled at her reflection in the mirror. *L'san, you're a genius!*

Gisela planned to arrive at the church just after Nadia, and the first person she saw was Nicolas. He was beaming with pride and anxious to see his bride. She told him how handsome he was, and she straightened his tie. She had become quite fond of him, enjoying their conversations when he accompanied Nadia to Paris for the fittings. He had asked Gisela last month what she thought would be appropriate for the groom to wear, and she had been happy to share her advice. They spoke for a few moments and then he directed her to where she would find Nadia.

Although Gisela had attended a few of the fittings, this was the first time she had seen Nadia completely dressed in her gown. Her timing was perfect. Isabella and the attendants left for a moment to take care of a few other details, and Nadia was alone, trying to attach the veil to the headpiece without success.

Gisela took a long look at the beautiful bride. She felt the tears starting to well in her eyes, but managed to hold them back from falling down her cheeks. "You'll take his breath away, Nadia. It's perfect, just perfect." Gisela saw that she had a dilemma with the headpiece. "Here, you have to start with the hooks at the back and work forward," Gisela said, and finished it for her.

"It's these nails, Madame Trist! I should have just asked for a manicure, but my friends convinced me to have a set of nails put on. They wear them all of the time, but I'm not sure I can! Imagine me trying to type with these!" Nadia held up her ten fingers in a helpless kind of way. Gisela laughed, but Nadia was completely serious about her dilemma. Gisela assured her that she would get used to them, or she could have them made shorter.

Next, she helped her put on her gloves. Nadia wasn't certain about wearing gloves until Gisela asked her, "Just how many women do you know that have perfect elbows?" She explained to Nadia that the focus during the ceremony would be on the back of the bride and groom. After Nadia thought about it, she agreed that it was important. *Madame Trist had taught her so many things about fashion and style.*

Gisela stepped back and looked at Nadia. "You're glowing!"

Then, Gisela presented her with a gift. "Oh, Madame Trist, you've done too much already. I just can't..."

"It's not from me," she said as she smiled playfully.

Nadia opened the little black velvet box. Inside was a note from Nicolas that read: *One year from today, to celebrate our first anniversary, will you meet me in Paris? Your loving husband, Nicolas.*

Nadia smiled. *Paris.* Her new favorite city. Nicolas had traveled with her for every fitting, and after each appointment, they spent the remainder of the afternoon as tourists. They had come across an elegant hotel near the Eiffel Tower, and decided that one day they would honeymoon there. They had already both agreed to postpone their honeymoon until they could afford to enjoy a week in Paris.

Under the note was a beautiful pearl bracelet, completing the set of pearls Nicolas had given her last night. "I can't believe it; he's spoiling me!"

Gisela clasped the bracelet over her glove on her left wrist. "It's just lovely, Nadia. I'm so happy for you and Nicolas." Gisela hugged her and decided she better leave and take her seat in the chapel.

"Madame Trist? Wait. I want you to know how much you mean to me. You've taught me so many things, and although you've been my boss, I think of you as my..." Nadia paused and thought for a moment. "...friend. In fact, you are my *best friend.*"

Gisela was moved by the feelings Nadia expressed to her. Tears welled in her eyes again as she thought of her friendship with Maritza. She reached out for Nadia and held her little friend silently for a few moments until she regained her composure. "Well, then, don't you think it's time you called me Gisela?" They both began to laugh through their tears.

"No, no, don't cry. You'll ruin your makeup," said Nadia.

"Me? You're the one getting married!" They both laughed again and found themselves relaxing in their newly defined relationship.

"I really must go now. It's almost that time. I love you, Nadia."

"I love you, too, *Madame Trist*," Nadia said, laughing. "Oops, I already forgot...*Gisela*."

Gisela grinned. "Okay, *Madame Schiller*."

"Gisela?"

"Yes?"

"Thanks for being here with me."

"I wouldn't miss it for the world."

"One more thing." Nadia looked at Gisela. "You remembered that I love lavender."

She noticed. "Of course I remembered." Gisela winked at her and walked out the door.

Gisela passed Isabella as she was coming up the stairs to let Nadia know it was time for the ceremony. They introduced themselves, having only spoken over the telephone. Gisela hugged Isabella and told her how beautiful she thought Nadia was in her gown. After wishing her well, Gisela continued down the steps until she ran into Hula.

"Well, Madame Trist. How nice to see you again. I was just on my way up to..."

Gisela motioned for Hula to turn around.

"Well, I never!" Hula turned around and Gisela followed her down the remainder of the steps. *There was no way she would allow Hula to ruin Nadia's day.*

"Actually, Mrs. Schiller, Nadia's not taking any visitors right now. In fact, she's about ready to come downstairs herself. Don't you think it's time for you to be seated?"

Hula stormed off and waited for her turn to be escorted up the aisle.

Gisela spoke with Nadia's father and congratulated him. He thanked her for everything she had done for Nadia. "She's my little girl," he told her with tears in his eyes. He started to cry and reached for his handkerchief. Gisela hugged him, and he saw how warm and caring she was to others. *No wonder my daughter is so fond of you.*

George regained his composure and introduced her to Alexander.

"I've been looking for you, Madame Trist." Alexander said. Nadia had insisted that she be seated with her family and that he personally escort her up the aisle. Gisela took Alexander's arm and he seated her near the front of the chapel with the other family members. She was touched to find herself sitting so close to the bride and groom. *Oh, Nadia. You're so thoughtful.*

She had one last thing to do before the wedding. When she was able to catch Nicolas's attention, she smiled and winked at him, and he knew his beautiful bride had received his gift.

Anna Lese and Marcella had joined Nadia, and they were chatting and giggling like they did when they were little. When Mama came to the door, her friends decided to give her some time alone with her daughter.

Mama saw her daughter's reflection in the mirror. She always knew her girl was beautiful, but today she looked even more special, radiant, in fact.

"Mama, what do you think?" Nadia twirled around just as she had when she was a young girl playing dress-up with her mother's clothes.

"Oh, Nadia, you look like an angel. My little girl is a beautiful, grown woman. Oh, baby, I'm so proud of you!" Mama began to cry.

Nadia moved toward her mother and hugged her. She loved Mama so much, and she was happy to be living nearby. "Mama, don't cry. I'm not going away. I'm just getting married."

"Just getting married? Nadia, that's a big step in a woman's life."

"You know what I mean, Mama. C'mon, only happy tears today!" They both laughed as they left their embrace, taking one more look in the mirror and delicately drying their eyes before moving downstairs to the vestibule.

Nadia picked up her bouquet and inhaled the sweet rose fragrance. She followed Mama carefully down the steps. "Is Papa waiting for us there?"

Mama stopped her for a moment, and then told her to wait about two minutes and then come down the stairs. She kissed Nadia and went down the final steps to join the rest of the wedding party.

A short time passed, and Nadia could hear the organist begin to play her favorite hymn. She walked down a few more steps and saw Papa nod his approval for her to join him.

Mama was walking down the aisle on Alexander's arm when Papa finally saw his daughter. He was already overwhelmed with how beautiful his own bride was moments ago, and now his daughter stood in front of him, perfectly dressed and looking like royalty. He pulled out another freshly ironed handkerchief, and Nadia tried to help him to wipe away the tears, but they just kept coming. Looking at his beautiful daughter reminded him of his own bride some thirty years ago.

Papa told her how beautiful she was and how much he loved her. He kissed her forehead and lowered the whisper veil over her face. Together they smiled and took a deep breath. The music changed and they watched as Anna Lese and Marcella walked gracefully up the aisle and stood to the left of where Nadia would stand and take her vows.

Nadia took Papa's arm and they started down the aisle. She realized after walking a few steps that he had decided to leave his cane in the vestibule and walk without it.

The small church was filled with candles and gorgeous, fragrant roses. Nadia had accepted Madame Trist's offer to provide the flowers for the wedding and reception. Gisela knew that Nadia loved sweetheart roses and made sure to include them in the bouquets and arrangements.

Nadia had lovingly saved all of the roses that Nicolas had given to her over the past year, and as the bride requested, those petals were scattered on the white carpeted path to the altar.

On her way up the aisle, Nadia winked at young Oliver and grinned as he winked back at her and gave her the thumbs up. She was thrilled that his aunt had agreed to bring him to the wedding. Ever since Nadia befriended the young boy on the train, both she and Nicolas dedicated one evening each week to spend time with him and help him with his reading.

Nicolas thought he was prepared to see Nadia, but he was dazzled by his bride's grace and beauty. He smiled at her as she approached him. By the time she was standing with Papa, just a few feet away from him, he felt his heart beating rapidly. *I love this woman!*

Hula kept her promise to her son and remained silent throughout the ceremony. Oskar knew she would behave because losing her son would kill her. For all the evilness in Hula, the one thing she did right was to love her son. Any sign of disgrace today would end their relationship permanently. Instead, she had purchased the most expensive dress she could find and prepared herself to smile and be cordial, to be photographed, and to act joyful throughout the festivities.

After all the drama and anguish leading up to this wedding, she watched quietly as her son took his vows to love, honor, and cherish this girl. What he saw in her, however, still bewildered Hula. But, for now, her son seemed happier than ever before. And her husband had made love to her last night for the first time in a year. On top of that, he had promised her a trip to Venice next month if she kept her mouth shut at the wedding.

For now, that was enough to buy her silence and make Hula very, very cooperative.

The End

Made in the USA